Praise for Ben Dolnick's

THE GHOST NOTEBOOKS

"Dolnick [has a] keen eye for detail and [a] penetrating ear for dialogue." —*The New York Times*

"Carefully crafted prose, subtle allusions, close observation and a cleverly presented theory of what the ghosts in question might want from humans. . . . A grown-up contemporary take on [a] haunting." —*The Florida Times-Union*

"A missing fiancée and a haunted house in the Hudson Valley are at the enigmatic center of Ben Dolnick's *The Ghost Notebooks*, but the real mystery is how well we know those closest to us." —*Vogue*

"Immersive. . . . Dolnick [gives] familiar motifs a contemporary sensibility in this ghost tale, love story, mystery, and bildungsroman." —*Publishers Weekly*

"In this compelling mix of love story, detective story, and ghost story, [Dolnick] takes a haunting look at what might follow life." —*Booklist*

Ben Dolnick

THE GHOST NOTEBOOKS

Ben Dolnick is the author of the novels *At the Bottom of Everything, You Know Who You Are,* and *Zoology.* His work has appeared in *GQ* and *The New York Times* and on NPR. He lives in Brooklyn, New York, with his wife and daughter.

bendolnick.com

THE GHOST NOTEBOOKS

THE

GHOST

NOTEBOOKS

. . .

Ben Dolnick

VINTAGE BOOKS

A DIVISION OF PENGUIN RANDOM HOUSE LLC

NEW YORK

FIRST VINTAGE BOOKS EDITION, JANUARY 2019

Grateful acknowledgment is made to University of California Press c/o Copyright Clearance Center for permission to reprint an excerpt from "On Some Other Planet You May Be Right" by Yehuda Amichai, from *The Selected Poetry of Yehuda Amichai*, translated by Chana Block and Stephen Mitchell. Reprinted by permission of University of California Press c/o Copyright Clearance Center.

The Library of Congress has cataloged the Pantheon edition as follows:
Names: Dolnick, Ben, author.
Title: The ghost notebooks / Ben Dolnick.
Description: First edition. New York : Pantheon Books, 2018.
Identifiers: LCCN 2017010133 (print). LCCN 2017013339 (ebook).
Classification: LCC PS3604.O44 (ebook).
LCC PS3604.O44 G48 2018 (print). DDC 813/.6—dc23
LC record available at https://lccn.loc.gov/2017010133

Book design by Anna B. Knighton

Vintage Books Trade Paperback ISBN: 978-1-101-97161-1
eBook ISBN: 978-1-101-87110-2

www.vintagebooks.com

Printed in the United States of America
10 9 8 7 6 5 4 3 2 1

For Elyse and Nishant, handrails in the dark

Look, just as time isn't inside clocks
love isn't inside bodies:
bodies only tell the love.

— *Yehuda Amichai*

PART ONE

. . .

Buried in this small family graveyard are Edmund and Sarah Wright, as well as their eldest child, William. What do you notice about the gravestones? Can you read what's written on them? How do you think these stones might have looked when they were first placed in the ground, more than a hundred years ago? We ask that you not touch the graves, but please feel free to write a message to the Wrights (let your imagination run wild!) and to place it in the box.

1

Let me explain, first of all, that I was never one of those people who believed, even a little bit, in ghosts. I knew people who did—people with office jobs and shoe inserts and wallets stuffed with sandwich punch cards—and I could never quite hide my bewilderment when I realized that they weren't kidding.

Even Hannah was ghost-curious, although she wouldn't admit it. She used to ask sometimes, in her *I promise I won't think less of you* voice, whether I'd be willing to sleep alone in a cemetery (many of these conversations took place during bleary predawn taxi rides, since our route to the airport happened to pass a town-sized cemetery near our apartment). "You wouldn't be at all scared?" Of course I'd be scared, I'd say, but what I'd be scared of would be that meth addicts might stab me, or that I'd die of frostbite, or that I wouldn't get any sleep because I'd be using a rock for a pillow.

This all feels bizarre to think about now, obviously, but if I'm going to tell you this story then I need to recreate my state of mind from before I knew anything about ghosts, or death, or anything, really. Which means, among other things, revisiting a part of my life that makes me want to curse and weep and pound my forehead with regret. But I can handle it. I'm fairly sure I can handle it.

I'll start with the night a couple of years ago when we were still living in our big, weird apartment in Astoria and Hannah suggested, in a voice not much different than if she'd been proposing an answer in a crossword puzzle, that we move upstate to a town neither of us had ever heard of.

"Look," she said, turning her laptop toward me.

DIRECTOR, EDMUND WRIGHT HISTORIC HOUSE
—Hibernia, NY

The Director of Wright Historic House (WHH) lives on-site in a beautifully preserved home from 1750, where he/she is responsible for maintenance of the property as well as the development and implementation of programs for schools and for the general public. Applicant must have background in museums, strong knowledge of 19th Century American history, as well as love and appreciation for the Hudson Valley area. Familiarity with maintenance of "unique" homes a plus.

" 'Unique' isn't a good thing, when they use it like that," I said.

"We could try it. Just see what it's like."

"I don't want to know what it's like."

"I'm going to email them."

"Do whatever you want," I said, standing up to gather some dishes I had no intention of washing. The windows were open and a fire truck was screaming its way up Twenty-fourth Avenue. This was the middle of May, a part of the year in New York when the smells have begun to stew and no one can believe that spring, all of it, was that one pleasant week in April. Hannah and I were in a relationship tunnel, and it wasn't at all clear to either of us that we'd get out of this one. The problem—one of the problems—was that we'd been together now for three years and she, at twenty-nine, had decided, without ever quite saying so, that we either needed to get married or break up.

Our fridge had become a collage of other people's "Save the Date" cards; our credit card bills went all to flights to cities we didn't want to visit where we sat sulking in folding chairs and pretended to be surprised when the bride appeared. I knew that I could solve our problems by proposing to her, and I knew that any remotely competent therapist would tell me that my reluctance had nothing to do with Hannah and everything to do with the fiasco of my parents' marriage ... but I couldn't. I might, I thought, be one of those people who never get married at all, who argue in a superior tone that the entire thing is an archaic and ridiculous institution. Or I might want very much to get married, just to someone other than Hannah, someone who would render the entire decision simple. Or maybe this present state—this muddled seasick doubtful queasiness—was just what it felt like for someone with my particular disposition to want to get married, and I should just get on with it.

The upshot, anyway, was that I avoided any subject even tangentially related to marriage and she ground her teeth at night and we both dreaded a creamy envelope in the mailbox like the black spot in *Treasure Island*.

"And what, I'd be a farmer?" I said from the kitchen. But another fire truck came roaring after the first one, so she could get away with pretending not to have heard me.

A component of our trouble—the thing that had taken our discontent from the back burner and poured it directly onto our laps—was that Hannah had, a few months earlier, been laid off.

It happened in winter, during an ice storm on a Friday afternoon: she called me crying from the break room and my first thought was that one of her parents had died. Is everything okay? No, she said, she was getting paid off. Paid off? Bribed? Not paid off, you fucking idiot, laid off! Laid off! Fired!

For two years she'd been working at the New-York Historical Society on the Upper West Side, standing an hour a day on the Q, eating eleven-dollar salads on Columbus Avenue for lunch. She'd been in their exhibit research department, writing signs and brochures and scripts for the guides to recite while they led tourists through exhibits about New York's ports and Abraham Lincoln. *America's most popular president, he is commonly associated with Illinois, where he made his mark as a lawyer, or Kentucky, where he was famously raised in a log cabin. Lesser known is the significant role that New York played in Lincoln's adult life.*

"This budget has just been a disaster for us," her boss explained; they were sitting in exactly the same positions as when he'd interviewed her. "I wish there were something we could do."

We were lucky enough—i.e., we still had enough money from my job and our savings and our families—that Hannah being laid off was not an imminent practical disaster: we would, for a while anyway, be able to pay the rent, and buy groceries without scrutinizing per-unit prices, and keep our gym memberships. But practical disasters, it turns out, aren't the only kinds of disasters. In the weeks and months afterward I came to understand, in a way I hadn't really when my acquaintance with people losing their jobs had been mostly via CNN headlines and Raymond Carver stories, why being laid off—even laid off from a job you've enjoyed, as opposed to needed—was always high on the list of stressful things that could happen to a person, and to a relationship. All of our tensions seemed now to have been dipped in a horrible radioactive juice; some nights I'd wake up at three in the morning with my legs sweating only to discover that Hannah was awake and sweating too—we were tangled together like sheets of damp saran wrap.

The first visible outgrowth of her being laid off was that she decided we should move (she spent a great deal of each day demonstrating, via job sites, that the only jobs available in her field happened to be outside the five boroughs). Whether to move was, we both understood, a proxy war over whether to get married. This meant that every job offer she came across led to a tense, desolate conversation about something like the housing market in Philadelphia or the lack of public transit in Atlanta. Many nights, as we sat eating dinner, lifting our forks to our faces with the blank, weary expressions of refugees, I had the feeling that we were actors in a play: *The End of Love,* now appearing at the Flea, acted with torturous realism by newcomers Hannah Rampe and Nick Beron.

I was working then, and had been for the last few years, as an assistant music editor. This meant editing music for movies, mostly mid-budget dramas that I would never have gone to see if I hadn't had anything to do with them. I was the assistant to a thin, bedraggled man named Jeremy who did all the actual creative work—the composing and the arranging and the watching and rewatching of the same eleven-second scene, trying to decide whether the emotional tenor of the moment called for an oboe or a muted trumpet. My contribution was more technical than musical; all day I sat in a semi-darkened room in Midtown, wearing expensive headphones, staring at a thirty-inch monitor, adjusting sliders by increments too small to see. My dreams often involved Pro Tools mixing boards, jagged multicolored graphs of sound files.

I'd come to editing as a concession—my plan had been (just as Jeremy's plan had been) to become a famous, or anyway a renowned, musician.

When I met Hannah I was just at the tail end of the period in which I believed this might actually happen. I'd made the regular station stops: a band that played talent shows in my Maryland high school, a series of tremblingly self-serious demos recorded on an eight-track, a biweekly appointment at the bar in Ann Arbor that paid in drink tickets. I played guitar and bass and piano and wrote songs that my dad, in a reflective mood, once said reminded him of the Cars.

And when I was a couple of years out of Michigan, I put out an album. This seemed, briefly, to be the success that I'd been dreaming of since I was twelve—a record label (now defunct) gave me actual money, I had an album release party, I went on a slightly depressing tour during which I put an incredible number of miles on my Camry. My mom, who'd never quite given up the idea that I should go to business school, sent me a congratulatory bouquet of balloons. Notices were somewhere between respectful and tautological ("Nick Beron's *Pushing Off* is a first album by a new singer-songwriter"). An online music magazine I'd only vaguely heard of named me one of that fall's artists to watch.

It's hard to say exactly when I decided this wasn't for me. Some of it was the money. And some of it was that I think I'd believed, without ever quite articulating it to myself, that to release an album was to ascend to a celestial plane from which you only returned in order to play sold-out shows at Radio City and to grant enigmatic interviews to *Rolling Stone.* That you could have an album out and still need to live with four roommates in Long Island City, that my life for the foreseeable future was going to consist of opening for friends' bands and sending out mass email reminders and playing shows for three people in the back rooms of Czech restaurants ... I peered down the road and I balked.

And music editing didn't feel entirely like a self-betrayal (although my dad, that year for my birthday, got me a T-shirt with the word "SELLOUT" printed across the chest). I was making decent money, I was using my musical abilities, I was occasionally attending premieres where people like Susan Sarandon and Jeff Garlin would waft thanks in my general direction. It was, of course, painful to see how little the world mourned the loss of Nick Beron the musician—there were no puzzled queries from disappointed fans, no pleas from record executives—but I was, occasional midnight pangs excepted, doing fine. Just as the function of most furniture is to fill up a room, the function of most jobs is to fill up a life.

By the time I met Hannah it had been a year since I'd last played a show, and I was just becoming practiced at describing myself, with just the right mix of irony and self-deprecation, as a "failed musician." I was twenty-six, with a beard I liked to scratch in moments of intense self-involvement, and round metal glasses whose lenses were perpetually in need of cleaning. I tended, a few minutes into any conversation, to find a way to mention the stars of whatever movie I happened to be working on, always in a tone that suggested that I wasn't entirely sure who they were.

"That must have been really tough," she said.

"Which part?"

"Well, you said you always wanted to play music. So deciding to go into editing must have felt, I don't know, like you were giving up on yourself, maybe. Is that bad to say?"

We had, I want to emphasize, met approximately twenty minutes before this conversation. I'd delivered versions of my music-industry spiel to at least a dozen people, and she was the first one who'd greeted it with anything other than nods of appreciation.

This was in the apartment of another assistant music editor, named Marisa. She'd invited a dozen people over for dinner to see her new place in Crown Heights (white-painted brick walls, sticky floors), and one of them happened to be Hannah, who she'd known at Oberlin. The rest of the guests were musicians, art teachers, personal assistants, one loud-voiced man who made sure that everyone knew he was just briefly touching down between stints in Berlin. This party was in January, so there was an air of picturesqueness: soap-flake snow falling outside, everyone in chunky sweaters.

When Hannah and I told the story of our meeting, we always stopped it at that first conversation about music—I'd given an obnoxious speech, she'd insulted me, and the rest was history. But I don't think I really took her in until later.

After dinner—we ate spaghetti with capers at a long table that was really a woodworking bench—an activity developed of people trying to light Italian cookie wrappers on fire. The girl who'd brought them said that if you rolled them into a tube and lit them, they'd float up to the ceiling. Hannah was sitting next to me, and we fumbled together with the lighter and the paper, laughing and correcting each other in the way of high school lab partners. She was tall (even sitting down you could tell) with a long neck, dark hair piled on top of her head, dramatic facial angles. Somehow most of her personality was concentrated in her eyebrows and mouth; her default expression conveyed a readiness to find something hilarious or ridiculous. "These things," she said, watching me fumble with the lighter, "are going to blow like Apollo 13."

"Apollo 13 didn't blow up. It reentered safely. That's why they made a movie about it."

"Good to know," she said. (She was highly attuned to the male blowhard, as a species, for reasons that became obvious as soon as I met her father.) She took the lighter from me and leaned over the table to light hers. We sat back. And while the cookie wrappers up and down the table rose in weightless silent majesty, ours tipped together on their sides and smoldered.

. . .

When Hannah and I were in our worst period of fighting, I'd sometimes marvel at the fact that we'd somehow gotten from lighting cookie wrappers to sleeping pressed against opposite edges of the bed without there ever being a single day you could point to and say, *There, that's where it happened.* This is a thing that I'm sure is obvious to everyone else but is never-endingly astonishing to me: that every change, every life, consists of nothing but a series of days. The shaky old wheelchair-bound man with a blanket on his lap, being hoisted out of the Access-A-Ride, was once a bulging-biceped, turnstile-leaping twenty-year-old, and the vessel that carried him all the way from there to here was no bigger than a box on a calendar.

Anyway, a few weeks after Hannah showed me the historic house job upstate—which I hoped she'd forgotten about, in the same way she'd forgotten about the Indian Museum job in Utah and the Civil Rights Museum job in North Carolina—we had the worst fight we'd ever had. Our neighbor, a fretful single mother named Tina, had knocked on our door to warn us that our air conditioner looked unbalanced, and this had led to an argument about whether I'd installed it right, which had led to an argument about whether she'd paid the electric bill, which had somehow, via a series of steps it would take a forensic pathologist to reconstruct, led to the two of us snarling and shouting at each other across the living room.

"You are so fucking afraid of everything and I don't even think you know it," she said at some point. "You just want to stay in the same shitty apartment living the same shitty life because it's easy and it's comfortable and I just can't fucking do it!"

"You are insane," I remember saying, with particular relish. "I didn't make you lose your job, I didn't make you sit around all day reading bullshit on Slate..."

"I can't believe I ever wanted to marry you," she hissed.

"Well, you're in luck," I said, and I stormed out. I slammed the door, which I don't think I'd really done since I was fourteen, and I was walking past the train station on Ditmars before it even occurred to me to wonder where I was going.

This was a Thursday night, just after eleven o'clock, still hot enough that it was like damp fabric pressed against your skin. This part of Astoria, on a summer weeknight, is like a stage set after hours. The Q was clattering overhead. An Asian woman in a dirty baseball cap was gathering bottles from a recycling bin in front of the GameStop. I wondered what would happen if I got mugged now, or murdered, how Hannah would find out. I wished I were smoking; I felt, from the heat of my breath, almost as if I were smoking. My hand was curled around my phone, the way it was perpetually, unconsciously, in half anticipation of the next dispatch from Hannah. Come home. Don't come home. I love you. I hate you. I pulled it out and turned it to Silent.

I would, I decided, stop in at Dino's (this was a bar where Hannah and I had gone a couple of times, remarkable in no way except for being five minutes from our apartment). Have a drink, fume for a while, then go home and face whatever was next.

But by the time I got the bartender's attention (he'd been turned around, watching baseball highlights), something strange had started to happen. The grain of the barstools and the glass of the bottles looked unusually vivid. I felt, before I'd even taken my first sip of Guinness, unusually spacious, as if a drug had just kicked in. I was happy.

A handful of men were seated farther down the bar, and a group of women at a table in the back; I wanted almost to call out to them. The air conditioning was already cooling the sweat on the back of my shirt. And I realized, touching the foam to my lips, what I was happy about: I was there as a single man. I laughed and knocked the bottom of my glass against the bar, toasting myself. For the first time in years, Hannah had ceased to be my problem. There would be logistics to sort out, details to negotiate, but I didn't need to worry about whether she'd call me or text me or if she'd still be mad at me tomorrow or if I'd still be mad at her. Our fight had burned through all that. I was free.

And so Dino's, which in any other circumstances would have been the perfect setting for an alcoholic depression, suddenly glowed. The bartender asked me if I needed another; blessings from a priest! The blue Bombay Sapphire bottle next to the green Jameson bottle: stained glass in a cathedral!

I could live my life as an editor, I could meet someone new, someone sane, I could be happy. How could I not have understood this? Hannah could go off and find some eager idiot who would propose to her on their first anniversary (this thought did give me a slight chill, I admit), and I would get an email from her in a decade and I'd look up from my desk and think, *Huh, I haven't thought about her in years.* This is how it happens: you can't imagine a person being out of your life until you can't imagine how she ever could have been in your life in the first place.

Hannah Rampe, Hannah Rampe, Hannah Rampe—I repeated her name until it became taffy, a name in the phone book.

The man next to me, I hadn't noticed, had been becoming increasingly interested in me over the course of my first couple of drinks. He was stocky, in his forties, with a band-aid on his thumb and glasses that he kept knuckling back in place. As soon as I gave any indication that I'd seen him he shifted over onto the stool next to mine. My reverie had found its audience.

Except he wasn't going to be an audience.

"Where is everybody tonight, huh? I mean yowie, what did I, miss a summit meeting? I'm kidding, my name's Len. How're you doing?" His breath smelled like beer and tortilla chips. He had the unmistakable shiftiness of someone who very much wants to tell you something.

And what that something was, it turned out, was his ex-wife. Well, actually she was still technically his wife, but they'd been separated now for nine months, and she had basically moved in with another guy, so they were as good as divorced. And could I even imagine what that did to his daughter, seeing her mom with this stranger? Eleven years old, an extremely sensitive girl, not your run-of-the-mill kid, this girl eats the ugliest strawberries in the container because she feels *bad* for them. Imagine how somebody like that would take it. And now *he's* the one who's not allowed to see her? *He's* the one? It's sick, is what it is. Mental perversion.

Every now and then Len paused to check if I needed another beer and to be sure I really understood the import of what he was saying. Occasionally he placed his hand lightly on my wrist, as if to make sure I wouldn't slip away.

And did I have any idea what dating was like now? Probably I did, nice-looking guy like me, but sheesh. Everything was all text me, message me, God forbid you should hear someone's voice, and double God forbid you should ever mention your ex, even if the whole point of why you were mentioning her was to explain why you were so glad to be out on this date at all. Usually this place was pretty good, though. One of the better places in the neighborhood. A week ago he'd talked to the bartender here (a lady bartender, not this one, ha-ha), and that was actually why he'd stopped in tonight, hoping she'd be working. Had I ever seen her, this little Asian girl, tattoo right here?

I don't know if it was that I'd passed a threshold of alcohol consumption while Len was talking, or if it was that his words had been perfectly calibrated to have this effect, but the bliss-conferring drug in me had now met its antidote. I didn't register until afterward that I was standing up, rifling through my wallet. I couldn't believe, actually couldn't believe, that until that minute I'd been thinking I was done with Hannah. Reality came storming back in on a thousand slippery legs.

I murmured apologies to Len, threw my money on the bar, and hurried back out into the heat and clatter of the street. I speed-walked back up Ditmars with that jitteriness in my legs, that sense of unspent adrenaline, like when you've nearly been hit by a car (and I did, in fact, come fairly close to being hit by an empty bus). It had been, according to the clock on my phone—on which I'd missed a call from Hannah, at 12:09 a.m.—a little more than an hour since I'd walked out our door. Two blocks from our corner I broke into a run.

I let myself into our apartment quietly, my heart kicking, expecting to find Hannah cross-legged, her jaw set, the computer glowing in her lap. I was braced for us to pick up right where we'd left off—shouts and curses and the realization that I really would be looking for a new apartment in the morning. Maybe she'd felt the same freedom I had, only without the reversal. Or maybe she'd already gone to her parents' and she'd been calling to tell me goodbye. I was ready (or I wasn't at all ready, but I thought I needed to be) for Hannah, the only woman I'd ever actually loved—that was so clear now!—to walk out of my life completely.

But the apartment was quiet—still and inhabited. I pushed

open the door to our bedroom and Hannah was under the sheets, on her side, her iPhone and Po Bronson's *What Should I Do With My Life?* arrayed next to her on the bed. Our bed. It could have been an illustration in a storybook called *Happy Home.* There was my bedside table and there was our fan humming softly away on the dresser and there was the painting of a bridge that we'd bought at that yard sale in Pennsylvania. There was what I should do with my life.

In gratitude I whimpered audibly, and she murmured something. She wasn't mad anymore; all that was done. Of course. She'd cooled off, she'd called me, she'd gone to sleep. The dramatic action, as ever, had taken place entirely in my skull cavity. I showered—twice as long as usual, to get the remnants of bar-stickiness off me—then climbed in next to her, trying not to disturb the mattress. She adjusted her body to let me hold her.

"I love you so much," I whispered into the warm white shell of her ear. My mouth, which had a few hours earlier been sputtering with fury, now felt newborn: Listerine and love.

"Mmnhh," Hannah said, pulling my arm over her, which was easier than rousing herself to the layer of consciousness at which she could have said something.

"I'm serious," I said. "I've been such an idiot."

"Mnnhhh," she said, more emphatically.

"I'm so sorry."

"You're drunk."

"I'm not. I love you."

She knocked my hand gently against her chest—a gesture of love and forgiveness and a plea for me to shut up and go to sleep. But I couldn't.

I shook her shoulder. "I don't care if you can't find a job here. We can move. I can quit. We can do anything."

I was Scrooge on Christmas morning; Len, muttering about

Asian girls while he plucked at his band-aid, had been my Ghost of Christmas Future. We could get married, have kids, make a life together. It wasn't too late.

"I'm serious," I said. "You should apply for that job." I could tell, from the angle of her head, that she was awake now, listening. The clock by our bedside said it was 1:16. "The one upstate. The house. We could just try it for a while. I can write music again. It would be an adventure."

She rolled onto her back. "I have a secret," she said, in the groggy voice of someone whose eyes are closed. For a terrible second my inner floor collapsed. She'd already found a new apartment. She'd been cheating on me. It was too late. No. She pressed my hand below her collarbone. "I applied on Tuesday," she said. "I have a phone interview next week."

. . .

What is this place, anyway?

The Wright Historic House is a museum dedicated to educating the public about Edmund Wright, the distinguished nineteenth-century writer and philosopher.

But WHH is much more than just another history museum. It also happens to be the very house where Edmund Wright and his family spent many years of their lives. When you walk in the door at WHH, you are literally stepping into history!

How long did the Wrights live here? Why Hibernia?

In 1866 Edmund Wright and his family moved to Hibernia from New York City, and they remained here in the house until Sarah's death in 1903.

The Wrights came to Dutchess County in search of a more "natural" life for themselves and their young children. Like many Americans of his era, Edmund Wright had become disillusioned with the increased mechanization and speed of modern life, and he hoped that in Hibernia he would discover a calmer, simpler way of being. (Just as many visitors to the area still do today!)

What did Edmund do while living at WHH?

An easier question to answer might be: What *didn't* he do while living at WHH? Edmund Wright can be thought of as the original Dutchess County "jack of all trades." In addition to teaching himself the basics of farming, and studying his beautiful natural surroundings, he wrote many works of lasting importance in philosophy and psychology, including his famous and unfinished encyclopedias, which you and your class can see in Wright's own handwriting right here in the museum!

While living at WHH, Wright published more than a dozen books, and tens of articles, not to mention writing thousands of pages of letters and journal entries. No wonder one publication of his era dubbed him the "human rotary press"!

Did he believe in the occult? I've heard strange stories about the house, and I am concerned.

Unfortunately, Wright, like many great figures throughout history, has seen his reputation negatively impacted by exaggerations and in some cases flat-out untruths. After the tragic death of the Wrights' eldest son, William, in 1869, Edmund, like many grieving parents, sought comfort by imagining an afterlife, but there is no reason to believe this brief flirtation impacted the rational pursuits for which he is known.

In the nineteenth century the line between "science" and "the supernatural" was not so clear as it is today. Even Charles Darwin, the father of evolution, expressed curiosity about what people might nowadays call "the occult." In many ways science was still like a toddler only just learning to walk!

As for stories that you or your students may have heard

about the house itself: imagine all that you would have seen if you had been alive for more than 250 years! Certainly this house has seen its share of sorrows, but it has also seen many joys. Our hardworking staff members have spent countless hours here at WHH, and we can assure you that none of them has ever heard anything more unusual than the occasional creak or the sound of a mouse in the walls.

Even as we respect the sometimes strong feelings and concerns of our visitors, we also feel it is important to maintain a sense of humor about the quirks that come with working in such a special place. That's why, if you enjoy your visit, we would like to invite you and your class to come back in October for our "Spooky Halloween Festival" to join in an all-in-good-fun day of storytelling and themed craft activities!

. . .

Winter 1985—New York—Age 4

You are sitting on the living room floor by the edge of the rug tangled white tassels your cat sits by your knee staring at a spot of sunlight on the floorboard he tilts his head you touch his neck he's purring not a sound but a buzz you close your eyes you try to purr then you feel by a shift in the floor that your dad is standing behind you there he is his legs you look up his hair standing up on the sides his blue sweatshirt his socks with the hole in the toe he sips too loudly from a black mug American Academy of Ophthalmology his glasses hold white squares of light that move when he moves he says and what are you doing with this beautiful day my darling no matter what you answer he's going to say that's a lovely thing for a little girl to do he'll lean over smell of coffee and morning and rough cheeks and then he does he leans over the cat darts off the buzz is gone you are sitting on the living room floor . . .

2

Hannah's phone interview led to an in-person interview led to a job offer with what might have been, if we'd been in a more skeptical frame of mind, alarming speed. But the force of my barstool conversion did not, surprisingly, dissipate in the weeks afterward. Breaking out of a relationship tunnel is every bit as astonishing, and every bit as convincing, as being stuck in one.

I told Jeremy, my boss, that I was leaving even before Hannah had officially been offered the job. He didn't seem so much furious, as I'd feared he would be, as mildly annoyed, as if I'd mislabeled a clip. We were wrapping up one movie, starting on another in a few weeks. "Hey, look, it's your call," he said. "Into the great blue yonder. I hope it works out. Just get me back that cut by the end of next week."

The decision to propose to Hannah, finally, hardly felt like a decision at all. What we'd been having was the storm before the calm; I'd seen friends go through it, packing up their clothes, going on internet dates, and then six months later standing hand in hand with their old girlfriends with tears of joy in their eyes. It was part of the ritual. I proposed at a tiny French restaurant in the East Village that was, despite the vanishing waiters and the wobbling chairs, our favorite place in the city. It was narrow and hot and the tables, lit by flickering tea lights, were so close together that you touched elbows with the strangers next to you.

It was the sort of place where couples were always having to disentangle their hands in order for the waiter to set down the food.

Something they don't tell you about proposing is that the act itself, even in cases of minimal suspense, is fairly awkward; directors cut to the woman's string of ecstatic *yes*es at precisely the moment when, in actual life, you, kneeling like a knight, sweating behind your knees, realize that this, the most meaningful speech of your life so far, is unfolding as a series of sentence fragments and saliva swallows. Hannah pulled me to my feet—I lost my balance and came uncomfortably close to tipping over our neighbors' table—and we kissed, standing, while everyone in the restaurant clapped and cheered.

Moving, after this, was nothing. There were still times in the middle of the night when I'd roll onto my back and think *the rest of our lives* or *health insurance,* but these were residue, bubbles working their way out of the system. Suddenly there were as many reasons to marry and to move as there had been, a couple of months earlier, to stew and to stay.

The Wright House only asked for a one-year initial commitment, for one thing (in winter the museum was only open a day or two a week); it would be our rite of passage, the threshold we passed through on our way to married life. And I was, the more I thought about it, convinced that the thing that had throttled my musical ambitions had been the city. How could I possibly have honed my craft in a place where the guy next to you on the train is on his way to Lincoln Center to play with Wynton Marsalis?

"It can be your Bon Iver cabin," Hannah said one night.

"I'm going to pretend you didn't say that."

This would, anyway, be my period of professional woodshedding and personal nonsense dispensing. Hannah would get some experience at running something, maybe finally do some writing. We would learn what it meant to live together—to rely on each other—as an actual couple, instead of as two vaguely hostile roommates.

"I can't wait to use the fireplace."

"I've always thought I could be someone who gets into birding."

"We should buy a hammock."

"We should buy hiking boots."

Some of our readiness to leave may have been New York's doing too; no city has ever been so cooperative in providing exit music for the uncertain. There was, one night on the N train, a puddle of Spam-colored vomit spread from pole to pole, with shoe prints. There was a deep, gut-rumbling alarm that sounded from the power plant near our apartment for an hour one morning. There was a prune-sized cockroach that skittered out from behind the coffee machine. Vomit, power plants, cockroaches: I leave the city to you; I'll be with my beloved and my guitar on a fifteen-acre farm.

Hannah and I drove two hours up the Taconic for her in-person interview on a sun-scrubbed Thursday. The scenery nailed its role: in Hannah's old college Volvo we sped through a crazy dark bounty of trees, over gleaming reservoir lakes, past hay bales and wooden fences and sculpture-still pecan-colored horses.

"Smell that," Hannah said, rolling down the window.

"I know," I said. "It's crazy. I wonder if they put drugs in the air."

Unless Hannah had been assaulted during the interview (it was conducted, at the house, by a sixtysomething board member whose main concern was whether Hannah knew of any art museums in the city that might be interested in giving his niece an internship), I don't think either one of us would have considered her turning down the job. The remoteness of the museum, the lack of visitors, the apparent lack of other candidates—these were, we hardly even needed to assure each other, not problems at all: they were challenges; they were curiosities; they were virtues in feeble disguise. A mind made up is a formidable thing.

. . .

How can I tell you about the Rampes?

Our last night in the city—this was the end of August; the only things left in our apartment were an AeroBed and a box of Thin Mints—we had dinner with Hannah's parents. It was hot but not gruesome, an emptied-out, leave-work-early-and-sit-dazed-on-a-boulder-in-Central-Park feeling to the city. We had dinner with the Rampes once a month or so, but this was only the second time we'd seen them since getting engaged, and they were determined to make it momentous: a send-off, and also a compensation for the last time, which had been the kind of hard-to-pin-down disappointment that was Hannah's parents' specialty.

The Rampes didn't like me; this was the simplest, and maybe the most accurate, way to put it, but it wasn't the way Hannah and I tended to put it, when we put it any way at all. *It isn't that they don't like you, it's that* . . . It was that they'd seen Hannah's older sister, Megan, go through such a series of relationship disasters (at thirty-three, she'd been divorced already, and was now living in Providence with a man they were fairly sure had stolen Terri's pain pills from the medicine cabinet). Or it was that they didn't know what to make of my sense of humor (Hannah's dad, Bruce, grimaced whenever people other than himself made jokes, as if he were recovering from a punch to the abdomen).

In any event, our get-togethers tended to be festivals of still-born conversations and strained smiles. My charms, which had paid my way through most of my life, were not accepted here.

Terri was in her early sixties, thin and unsure of herself. She had dark hair and Hannah's nose and a quick, quiet voice. She was always calling Hannah because she needed help signing into her bank account, or because she was certain she'd bought theater tickets but somehow they'd disappeared. She'd worked in publishing, before Hannah was born, then in PR, then doing research for a historian ("I always thought I was *just* about to find what my thing was going to be"), but now she seemed mainly to make plans, and to worry.

Bruce was an eye surgeon; this was the first, and possibly the only, thing he thought you needed to know about him. He took yearly trips to Tanzania, where he performed free surgeries for village kids who then hung grinning from his biceps in photos. He jogged a loop of Central Park each morning, and was under the impression that their building's doorman ("That's all you running today, Mr. R?") was personally fond of him. He had a full head of gray hair and pink skin and he interacted with everyone, including his offspring, in a way that managed to convey *I'm going to do you the favor of listening hard to what you're saying right now, but please understand that the meter is running.*

The Rampes had lived for thirty-five years in the same apartment on the Upper West Side, and they were both dedicated to New York in a way that bordered on the cultish. They knew someone in the city who excelled at every human endeavor: the best tailor, the best butcher, the best off-Broadway theater director, the best guy to talk to if you needed curtains. When they went on vacations—every couple of years they took a two-week trip to somewhere like Morocco or New Zealand—it was only to refill their store of fanaticism. "Is there a rule against putting ice in the water?" "You know what your mother pointed out after we'd been there a couple of days? No one was sitting in the parks! They're just empty."

When Hannah first told her parents that we were engaged, they had only just absorbed the fact that we'd be moving upstate. Terri said, "Wait, you weren't on speaker. What did you say?"

"Nick and I are engaged."

"To be married?"

"Yes."

I heard Bruce's voice in the background. "Since when?"

They took us out to a celebratory dinner at Il Buco (the best Italian restaurant) that was slightly, but only slightly, more successful than the phone call. Bruce, after some conversation about when we wanted the wedding to be (we didn't know) and whether we thought it made sense to be taking on so much change at once (we did), got into an argument with the waiter about whether there were enough shrimp in his pasta. This was how nights with them went: awkward jousting, expensive food, and then Hannah, at some point afterward, asking, "Why can't they just be *normal* with you?"

But her parents were not, Hannah would regularly insist, as difficult as they seemed. They'd come around. They were just protective. They loved her absurdly. And it was true; they did. My own parents, by comparison, were as involved in my life as an uncle and aunt. (My mom, when I told her that Hannah and I were engaged, said, "Oh, that's great news. We just *love* her, *love* her," and then asked if she could call me back because she was about to pull into the garage.) So there was something I envied, for all the unpleasantness, in the closeness of the Rampes. They regarded Hannah as in need of special protection, and they were going to be the ones who provided it. I even understood why.

This is a tricky area; I feel, edging up to it, like I'm walking a crumbly-edged trail on the lip of the Grand Canyon. I can't tell how much of this is hindsight, but the story fluoresces now, it seems like the most important thing I ever learned about the Rampes.

In any event:

When Hannah was just out of Oberlin, she had a kind of breakdown. She didn't tell me about this until we'd been together for about a year, and even after she had told me about it she only ever referred to it in the most general terms ("When I was having a hard time after college"; "When that stuff happened"). It was a chapter excised from the history books, reduced to a single uninformative paragraph.

What had happened, so far as I could tell, was that an ordinary but stressful set of experiences—the sudden death of a cousin, a bad boss, some complicated falling out with a friend—had all come in quick succession, and she had, in a way she'd never done before, cracked. Skipping work to weep in bed. Going out to dinners with friends and then, partway through, feeling so suddenly and inexplicably terrified that she would stand up and run back to her apartment, her heart racing. For a while she couldn't sleep because she was afraid she'd stop breathing in the night, so she would call her parents and keep the phone next to her on the pillow. This was when she was living in the West Village with a roommate, working at a law office. There may have been mild delusions (she'd told me about her ceiling pulsating, her curtains seeming to flap at her), but some of these may have had to do with drugs: her roommate, seeing what a bad time she was having, had convinced her to take mushrooms, which had only pushed the meltdown into a new and direr phase.

The upshot was that she quit her job and broke her lease and spent a few months at home, trembling in bed, being dragged by her parents from one therapist to another, suddenly a child again at twenty-three, only more helpless than when she'd actually been a child. Bruce and Terri were at their best in a crisis, apparently. Cool washcloths pressed against her forehead. Cary Grant marathons on TMC. Bruce eventually got her an appointment with a psychiatrist he knew from med school, Dr. Blythe, and he ended up being the savior; he prescribed her a combination of pills and talk that, over the next couple of months, brought her to a state where she was exhausted but not miserable, and just as puzzled by what had happened to her as everyone else was. She found a new apartment. This was when she got her first job in a museum. By the time I met her you would never have guessed she'd had any sort of psychological trouble at all—she projected a capable, cheerful ease in the world; it would have been easier to believe that she'd founded a company in her twenties than that she'd had a breakdown.

But for her parents, of course, the memory was still close. To have watched your child collapse is to live the rest of your life on a partially frozen pond. So their wariness about me may have made a certain kind of animal sense. Their daughter had demonstrated the capacity for sudden plunges, and I had not yet proven myself capable of picking her up.

Anyway, that night in August, we grilled hamburgers out on the deck of their apartment and watched the sun set showily over New Jersey. Bruce and Terri were arguing in their repartee mode about Terri having forgotten to buy cayenne for the corn. Their dog, a fat black cocker spaniel named Mickey (who had a regimen of pills much more extensive than Hannah's), kept wandering between our ankles, hoping for scraps.

"A toast to your engagement ...," Bruce said, lifting up a strikingly full glass.

"And to starting to think about wedding dates and venues and all that fun stuff," Terri said, clinking carefully.

The main thread of conversation kept returning, despite Hannah's best efforts, to how much they'd miss us once we moved. Terri inched her chair closer to Hannah's and said, "You realize,

I hope, that you're going to have to call us the second you get there. I can't stand driving on the Taconic—after the last time I said I'd never do it again—and just thinking of you two with the car all loaded up and all these other drivers weaving around ..."

Bruce kept going inside to adjust the volume on the stereo—whenever conversation wasn't aimed at him directly, he kept himself in a state of restless bustle: making sure the burgers didn't need to be turned, plucking dead leaves out of the plants by the railing.

"A patient of mine has a house not far from Hibernia," he said, coming back outside. "Twenty-nine minutes—I looked it up. You ought to get together for a meal."

He was still wearing his blue biking outfit from a ride that afternoon; whenever he came near I got a whiff of low tide.

"I'm sure your seventy-year-old patient is dying to have dinner with his doctor's daughter and her fiancé."

(The word *fiancé* still had a certain unsheathed-blade effect on her parents.)

"He's fifty-nine, for your information," Bruce said, recovering himself.

"Wouldn't it be nice to know someone up there?" Terri said. "That's the part I always found scary about moving, the not knowing anyone."

We'd finished dinner, and I was in the kitchen refilling my water glass, mentally congratulating myself on having gotten through the night—in the pantheon of Rampe dinners, this had been fairly painless—when Bruce walked in behind me and let the door swing shut. I realized I'd been set up, stalked like a deer.

"So," he said, zipping and unzipping one of the pockets on his shirt. "You've probably noticed we're a bit stirred up."

"Are you?" I said. "I know this is a big deal."

We were standing a few feet apart, not quite looking at each other.

"Lemme just get to the point. Hannah's our priority. You don't understand what that means yet, but you will. Megan is too, of course, but you understand why this might all be a little more—intense, with Hannah."

I nodded solemnly.

He stepped closer and put his hands on the edge of the island and lowered his head, like a boxer between rounds. What he said next didn't sound like him; normally his voice had an eyebrow-wobbling, ironic quality—Hannah called it his *Oh do you?* voice—but now all smugness, all playfulness, was gone. He spoke quickly and quietly.

"You're taking her off somewhere, just the two of you, you're talking about getting married, things are feeling pretty good right now. I know you think you know her well, you guys have been together a few years, but I want you to know she's trickier than that. She seems very sure of herself, but that's taken work, that's not an accident. If this moving upstate doesn't work out, or if you decide, well, whaddaya know, maybe marriage isn't the thing, she'll take it harder than you can probably imagine. And you won't be the one who picks up the pieces." He cleared his throat, seeming to sense that he'd gone too far. "Look. Terri and I just want her to have a happy life, good husband, good family, all the standard stuff. We just want to be sure you get that."

I didn't know if I was being warned or cursed or what, exactly. My face was burning, and a part of me wanted to march out onto the deck and grab Hannah by the arm and storm out of these lunatics' lives forever. Instead I swallowed and told him that I understood.

"I'm glad," he said, putting his hand on my back and guiding us out into the living room. "That's very good."

We all said elaborate goodbyes in the front hall ("You'd better go already or I'll start crying," Terri said, already crying), and on the subway ride home, Hannah, resting her head on my shoulder, said, "What did my dad say to you in the kitchen?"

"Just to be careful on the drive, because of cops."

The next morning, thanks to nerves and a leak in our Aero-Bed, Hannah and I woke up before the alarm. I'd just had a dream involving climbing a sand dune. We lay for a few minutes in that cobwebby preverbal state, not talking. The light in the room, our soon-to-be-former bedroom, was blue; the street outside was the quietest I'd ever heard it.

"You feel like manifesting a move?" Hannah finally said. This was a phrase I'd almost forgotten—we'd heard a blond-dreadlocked woman say it a few years before on the phone in an incense-stinking birthstone-and-beads store on Bleecker Street; she'd been manifesting a move to Brazil, wondering when the universe would start sending her signs of compliance.

"I do," I said. My heart, possibly just for reasons of morning-systems balkiness, had started knocking around in my chest like a trapped squirrel. "Do you?"

"I do," she said, sitting up. "The vibrations have commenced."

. . .

Once there was a man named Edmund Wright. He lived in New York City, when it was much smaller than today but still a very big city. He had a happy family and he liked his job, which was writing books, but he always had a bad feeling that something was going to happen to his oldest son, William, whom he loved more than anything in the world. Sometimes he would have dreams where William would fall out a window. Sometimes he would just be sitting at his desk and out of nowhere he would imagine William getting trampled by a horse.

So one day, when Edmund had had enough of being scared, he decided to move his family out of the city and up to a little town called Hibernia. He was sure that William would be safe there. And sure enough, life was good in Hibernia! Edmund and his family ate vegetables from their garden, and went for walks in the beautiful woods. "I feel as sturdy as one of these oak trees!" said Edmund. For the first time in years, he had some peace of mind.

But one foggy fall evening, Edmund decided to go into town to visit a friend. He hitched up his horse and carriage *[show Carriage Illustration # 1]* and he told his family that he would be back in time to say good night. But his horse had only taken a few steps when Edmund heard a cry and felt his carriage stop in its tracks. What Edmund hadn't seen, because the evening was dark and the fog was thick, was that, just as the carriage was pulling away, William had been climbing up the wheel to give him a farewell kiss. William had been pulled into the spokes and now his lifeless body lay in the road. "No!" Edmund cried. "My boy! My beloved boy!" But it was true: William was gone.

Edmund and his family lived in Hibernia for many years afterward, and they still had three wonderful children *[show Wright Family Portrait #2]*. But secretly, Edmund never forgave himself for William's accident. "Why?" he would ask. "Why did I ever leave New York?"

And sometimes at night, when no one else was awake, William's ghost would appear by Edmund's bed, looking just as he had when he was alive, only much paler now and floating a few inches off the ground. William's ghost never said a word—he just moved across the room like a cold patch of fog. "I'm sorry!" Edmund would cry out, waking up his wife. But the ghost wouldn't speak. It would just move closer and closer—and then, just before it disappeared, it would lean over and, with its icy lips, give Edmund a farewell kiss.

Discussion questions:

• Do you think Edmund really saw William's ghost late at night, or was it just his imagination? [Call on three to four students.]

- Why do you think Edmund said he should never have left New York? [Call on three to four students.]

- Have you ever had a bad feeling you couldn't explain? Did you act on that feeling? Why or why not? [Call on three to four students.]

...

You are standing in spotted shade you are facing your husband he is almost your husband your friends your family are sitting in chairs on logs they are fanning themselves your grandmother tiny and ancient is perched in the first row the rabbi is going on too long he made a joke you can only tell because everyone is laughing so you laugh your almost-husband laughs squeezes your hands you look down your toenail polish is red your feet are white his shoes are black and then the rings spinning past knuckle-flesh onto bare fingers his palm is damp his eyes are brown with darker flecks you kiss like you've each been ship-wrecked from somewhere music starts and even your grand-mother is standing you are walking back down the aisle you just walked up you don't know how many minutes it's been someone hands you a piece of chicken on a wooden stick people with red faces hug you and ask you how you feel say how beautiful that was absolutely lovely absolutely perfect your dad is standing waiting to say something your mom is crying laughing trying to fix the contact in her left eye while your sister all in purple holds her scarf your husband says are you OK kissing you again each of you now holding narrow glasses of champagne you're crying and you say to him of course I am I'm happy I'm supposed to be crying and he kisses you again because the photographer missed the last one you are almost certain this is why you're crying you can't think of a single thing that's wrong you could almost swear it . . .

3

Welcome, welcome! How you guys doing? Hannah? Nick? Donna McCullough. Founding board member, education specialist, all-purpose pain in the you-know-what. We spoke on the phone. The board president, Mike, was supposed to be here, but he got hung up at work. You hit any traffic? Hit any deer? That's a joke, this isn't when you'll hit deer, that's more like October.

"... Isn't it good-looking? Remind me when we get inside and I'll show you some pictures of how it was when we bought it. I swear you would have thought it was a completely different house. To give you an idea, this whole porch was red, like new-convertible red. So we scraped and scraped, and there was the dark green, still underneath. And it's not like we got everything perfect. We tried to get close—they have historic color 'experts' who'll come out and consult with you for about a million dollars—but with a job like this you basically have to accept that you're only ever going to get a close approximation. It hasn't been repainted since ninety-nine, anyway. That's a grant you might think about applying for.

"... So I've just got to say how glad I am that you guys are here together. I think that's great. I know some people have probably been bitching to you about it, saying, *Oh, what are we, a honeymoon destination?*, but the way I see it: How'd it go, Jim living here on his own? You think that might have, I don't know, made things a little harder for him?

"... You're not in museums, right? Remind me what you do?

"... Oh, I think that's great. My mother was too. Played piano in church every Sunday for thirty-seven years, First Methodist right over on Cold Spring.

"... Now, you feel how cool the air is inside? That's not AC, that's because when they built houses like this they actually had to think about things like which way the windows were facing and how high the ceilings were and everything like that. We could use some more of that, instead of these places you drove past on your way in, where they've got 'home theaters' and indoor pools and you're just thinking, *Do you people even care that you live in one of the top ten beautiful settings in New York?*

"... That was the problem with the guy we interviewed last month, in my opinion. He didn't seem to notice the word 'historic' in 'historic house,' so he thought it was going to be all queen beds and hot showers and just basically a hotel where you got paid to stay. Which is another reason I pushed for you guys, because I could tell from your application you got it, you weren't going to go running the other way the first time a bat climbed in the window. Now just come on through here for a minute.

"... So this is the caretaker's apartment, which used to be a storage area. You can see it's got basically everything you'll need—bed, kitchen, a little bathroom, microwave, lamps, extra blankets and towels and things in here. There was still some of Jim's stuff in the dresser, believe it or not. I guess nobody ever thought to clean it out. Coming from the city this probably seems big to you. Did I tell you I have a cousin in New York? Brooklyn. Coney Island Avenue. Been there for twenty-five years. I'm hoping to take the train down there this January, after my knee surgery. That's why I'm slow going down the stairs.

"... See, that was another thing people kept saying, *Hey, she's from the city, she's never worked in a historic house before, wah wah wah,* but the way I see it is, having somebody not from Hibernia is a good thing. God forbid we hire somebody who's not all caught up in small-town crap from fifty years ago, or who knows a thing or two about marketing or big-time museum shows. Wouldn't want to actually risk building Edmund Wright's reputation a little bit, would we? Or gee, I don't know, fulfilling our actual mission as an organization?

"... Anyway, so this is your office here—not exactly state-of-the-art, but it does the job. And now we're into the museum—this is the famous study. We don't just let people wander in here, they have to be with an educator, mostly 'cause of the books. This was the kind of desk he would have had, with all these little drawers back here. He wouldn't have actually written with a quill, but kids like it.

"... Hmm? No. Most of the stuff in the house is what I call a 'genuine antique.' Same sort of thing the Wrights would have had, but not the actual stuff.

"... Now, did they tell you that I'm actually related to Wright? Seriously? Yeah, well, I shouldn't be surprised, I think it pisses 'em off, makes 'em feel like I'm trying to make some special claim to the crown, which I'm not. They tried to kick me off the board a couple of years ago too. Probably didn't tell you that either.

"Well, he was my great-great-grandmother's brother, so my great-great-granduncle. Oh yeah. I'm not one of the kooks about him, come here and talk a lot of nonsense, because my grandmother actually met him. She used to have Indian fights with her sisters back out in those woods. For us it's not just some story.

"... Well, it's a good question. When we first opened in ninety-two we had to focus mostly on the outdoorsy stuff, since people still had other associations with the house. We'd go do a walk in the woods, or we'd take people canoeing on the river. We still have a canoe out there if you want to use it, actually. It was like a camp. That was when I was director.

"Then, you know, next generation comes along, lots of school groups, and of course they can't do as much outdoor stuff, because insurance has gone nuts. So what do we do? We start doing more stuff in the house. Exhibits like the one we've got up now about nineteenth-century baking. But then you get these kids' parents refusing to sign permission slips, and they won't say why, but it's obvious if you've lived here for half a minute. So, short version, the board decides to hire a new director, makes me a 'special consultant.' Gotta pay your respects to the almighty dollar sign.

"... So let me just take you down to the basement for a minute, show you some of the mechanicals, before I turn the keys over and let you wander around a little. I'd show you around the woods—have you seen the family plot yet? Said howdy to old Edmund and Sarah?—except my knee is basically hanging together like this, so I shouldn't even be walking around this much.

"... Watch your heads. This is the furnace—you won't be needing that for another month at least. This is the fuse box, which unless you go plugging in, I don't know, one of those giant industrial blenders, you shouldn't have any problems with. This is the water purifier, and this is the little booklet for it. These beams—this is all powderpost beetle damage, which I've been trying to get the board to care about for years. You might see a little moisture on the foundation in this corner here ...

"... Well, thank you. It's called institutional knowledge, and I wish there were a little more of it, frankly.

"... That's the line out to septic. Oh, and we think that's where there used to be a coal chute.

"... All right, so I'll get out of your hair in a minute. I can see I'm making you a little antsy, Nick. No, it's okay. Hannah, you and me'll be seeing lots of each other, since me and you and Butch are basically the whole show right now. You can always call me if I'm not in and you have a question, or you can even come by sometime. Me and my sister are four miles down eighty-two, then a right on Hobb's Lane, then another right. Little brick house with the metal sunflowers out front.

"… Well, you're welcome. You're very welcome. My only advice is, remember this place is actually where Edmund Wright lived, no matter what kind of cheapo furniture we have, no matter what people do or don't know about him. He was an actual, brilliant guy, and this is where he slept and ate and excuse me but screwed his wife. So you're actually pretty lucky, living here. Don't let them trick you into thinking of it as just another creaky old house."

. . .

Those first few weeks at Wright felt like being on a reality show. Take two city people, whose lives for the past six years have been all subway platforms and bodega aisles, and plunk them down on a farm where the main daily excitement is the UPS truck driving by. Watch them realize, at four p.m. on a Monday, that the only person they've seen all day other than each other is the muttering bald man who came in wondering if the museum would buy his old silverware.

I realized, once we'd been there for a bit, that "upstate" is an absurdly inadequate term. I knew, from a handful of weekends and an excruciating number of trend stories, about the slice of upstate that was Brooklyn with a backyard—drinks in Mason jars, lights strung up between trees, cutely named cheeses. And I also knew about the pockets that were in a state of genuine collapse—casino disputes and pawn shops and bars where carbuncular men sat drinking at ten in the morning.

But I hadn't had the slightest idea about Hibernia's brand of upstate, which wasn't the least bit hip (the median age seemed to be fifty-plus) but also wasn't particularly desperate. It was just, in a way I hadn't quite known a town could be—there. Its main reason for being, its rallying cry, if it could have been bothered to have one, was: *Just let us go about our business, please.* There was a church where I'd never seen more than a few cars parked ("God Proved His Love When He Gave It Away"). A hardware store permanently advertising a special on mulch. Some not-especially-picturesque farms where cows stood in circles on muddy ground, chewing hay.

It was less a town, in the farmers' market and community theater sense, than a collection of houses that happened to be scattered along the same river. I don't want to give the wrong impression—the people we met at Peck's (a linoleum-floored general store where the employees, between customers, sat in white plastic chairs sighing at Fox News) were perfectly friendly, and there were undoubtedly all sorts of neighborly doings that we hadn't been there long enough to know about: there was a town grange, and a Lions Club, and various other social organizations I only partially understood. But there was a basic flintiness, an unsmiling nod from a pickup truck kind of spirit, that until then I'd associated more with New Hampshire or Maine than New York. The most reliable evidence we had of our neighbors' existence was the sound of distant gunshots.

Our house, the museum, was on an easy-to-miss road called Culver Lane. It stood back a ways on a hill, on fifteen acres of what had once been farmland, now woods and grass paths and half-collapsed stone walls. Sometimes, when there wasn't a school group, only one or two visitors came in an entire day; sometimes no one did. If you walked fifteen or so minutes from our back door, out across our property and then a couple of fields that belonged to a farmer who was never there—insects crackling all the time like stray voltage—you came to the Hibernia River.

The house itself was smallish, wooden, slightly shabby—its paint, sooty white, was crackling and peeling in strips like birch bark. The roof had asphalt shingles with green lichen spots. There was a narrow porch with a blackened metal plaque mounted between the windows: "Edmund Wright Historic House

Museum, Founded 1992, Hibernia, NY." There was a smell as soon as you got through the front door—smoke-cured wood and dusty books and possibly the faintest hint of dead mice.

You wouldn't, if it weren't for the plaque, necessarily know from the outside that it was a museum; you might just think this was an old farmhouse that school buses liked to park in front of occasionally. But inside there was a welcome desk with a stack of folded visitors' guides and a mug full of tree-bark pencils you could buy for two dollars each. There was a cash box and, on a little wooden stand, a copy of *The Selected Letters of Edmund Wright,* with him looking warily out at you from the cover. There were faded and peeling wall panels with curlicued quotes *("Oh, what happy hours and torments, what odysseys unwritten and invisible, have taken place within this study's sorry walls . . .")*.

We only learned about the house, what had happened there, from Butch, the museum's maintenance man. Butch was one of those men, of whom there seemed to be a surplus in Hibernia, who take stoicism just to the edge of scarecrow-hood. He was in his fifties. He wore a Carhartt jacket and a plain blue baseball cap and he stood noticeably straight. Hannah asked him one day while they were fixing the gutters what Donna had meant, about small-town crap from fifty years ago; if not for that conversation I think we could have gone the entire year without anyone bothering to tell us.

In 1958—decades after the Wrights were dead, decades before the county historical society bought the house and made it a museum—a man murdered his wife there. Possibly. They were George and Jan Kemp, the town doctor and his pretty wife, and Jan disappeared one winter and was never found. This was, apparently, the most scandalous thing ever to have happened in Hibernia. Butch's older brother had gone to school with the youngest Kemp daughter, so he'd known the family slightly, and he'd stared along with everyone else whenever George appeared in town. "For all anybody knows, she got ticked and took a bus to Buffalo," Butch said. "But the old folks still talk about it."

This, apparently, contributed to the museum's aura in Hibernia, half proud historic site and half place for high schoolers to prove their boldness by going up and pounding on the door. Hannah and I weren't particularly bothered by the story—to have lived in New York City for any length of time is to have accepted the idea that bizarre and horrible things have taken place in every room where you've ever set foot—but we were glad to know about it. Suddenly Donna's way of scurrying past the house's post-Wright history ("Oh, that's all just red meat for the loons") made sense.

But no one else ever mentioned the Kemps explicitly to us—I don't know if this was because not many people in town cared about the story anymore, or if it was wariness around newcomers. The closest people ever came was when the cashiers at Peck's or the waiters at the pizza place on 82 would ask how we liked living in "the museum," and there would be a mix of amusement and skepticism in their voices that meant they thought they knew something we didn't. We'd make a point to answer cheerfully ("It's like house-sitting for an insane uncle"; "It's like *Night at the Museum,* only much smaller"), and they wouldn't pursue it; they'd just smile and say, in a thinly encouraging voice, "Well, we're glad you're here."

But we actually *did* like living in the museum. There was a weird coziness to being there, at first, a playfulness, the way there would have been if we'd been camping or living on board a ship. The Kemps, the Wrights—they were jokes, myths, no more real to us than pterodactyls. We'd shout to each other laughing from another room to point out some new absurdity—a broken floorboard, a drawer stuffed with misprinted flyers. Neither of us had lived in a house since we were kids; apartments, it turns out, are very different things, psychologically. Houses—

especially old and creaky houses—are individuals, somehow; their fronts are faces, their closets are pants pockets. We went, after hours, on exploratory missions to the basement (dirt floor, stone walls, bare hanging bulbs). We put on overcoats and metal glasses from the costume closet and leapt out at each other. We read each other entries from Edmund's and Sarah's diaries. It turns out that if your significant other becomes the caretaker of a historic house and you move with her, then whether you like it or not you become the caretaker of a historic house too.

Our room, the caretaker's apartment, was off the back of the house, down a few steps from the display kitchen with its potbellied stove and plastic potatoes. Our room didn't look so different from a ground-floor apartment I'd lived in once—a double bed, a kitchenette, a much-faded area rug.

"Does our room feel," Hannah said, "a little bit like after a hoarder dies and they clean out his apartment?"

"I think the vibe I get is more sad-lonely-man-sitting-in-his-underpants," I said.

This was another thing about living there: so much more suddenly depended on our conversation. We were (because the wireless was crappy, and because there was only one spot upstairs that got a cell signal) each other's primary means of entertainment, a society of two. We would do impressions for each other, we would cook dinners that involved double-boiling and constant stirring.

"Oh, Edmund," Hannah said to me one night, in her *Masterpiece Theatre* accent. We were upstairs in the Wrights' bedroom, looking through the closet for an extra lamp. "Won't you make love to me right here on our four-poster bed?"

(The Wrights' bedroom, just to the right at the top of the stairs, was surprisingly spare, almost Shaker: a narrow bed, a wooden chair, a candle in a candle holder. I heard a woman that first week say to her husband, "Not a lot of fun you could have in here.")

"Sarah, dear," I said, "I've never been able to resist a woman in a bonnet." I lifted Hannah up like a mermaid (this was a back-endangering maneuver, to be attempted only on special occasions) and tossed her onto the bed—and this was how we discovered that Edmund and Sarah's mattress was actually just two garbage bags full of styrofoam peanuts.

"You two have already brightened this place way up," Donna said one day. "So much cheerier than Jim moping around. People are going to be coming back here in droves."

Donna had straight gray hair to the middle of her back, thick glasses, an almost lipless mouth; her T-shirts all said things like "You're Dang Right I Love History" and "Don't Blame Me I Voted For the Other Guy." She was an amateur potter, and she referred regularly to a hippie past. "Me and a girlfriend went to Paris once, almost got tossed in a French jail with these two real 'artistic' guys we were going around with, that woulda been fun." "That was back when I could still smoke. Now if I took one puff it would be *Sayonara, Donna, see you in a week.*"

"You guys have a picnic back by the river yet?" she said. "Oh, you gotta do that before it gets cold. Take a bottle of wine, walk down a ways, climb up on one of the big boulders. Hell, you can even go skinny-dipping, if nobody's fishing."

One night we did—we canoed down to a swimming hole, and then we left our clothes on a rock and took turns leaping—and then we walked back to the museum in beach towels, barefoot, dripping, quietly amazed at our luck.

"You're looking at me weird," Hannah said, smiling.

"I'm feeling weird," I said.

Back in our room I cooked spaghetti while Hannah sat on the bed by the open window, drying her hair. "I'm glad we came here," I said, but the words were just the clattering lid on a brimming pot of feeling. *We've really started on our life together*—that was closer to what I meant. *Someday over geriatric cups of tea we'll remember when we lived in a museum, we'll interlock liver-spotted hands and say, "Remember how steep those stairs were? Remember the time we saw a fox by the picnic table? Remember the giant rusty front-door key?"*

Especially at night, the air in our room had a kind of root-cellar coolness. The racket of crickets and frogs and God knows what else swelled until it pressed right up against the house. We felt not just alone on the property but alone on earth.

In bed we'd have conversations that were different from the ones we'd had in the city, more private, stranger. "Have I told you how much I showered when I was in middle school?" Hannah said one night. "Like three times a day. At least. I was obsessed with thinking I smelled. I think Megan must have been the one who freaked me out about it. She used to make this face when I sat near her. I was always sniffing myself, pretending I was just looking down at my shirt. My skin was all red, from scrubbing. My dad would yell at me. We had these green loofah things that were always coming unspooled." We stayed up—midnight actually felt like the middle of the night in Hibernia—telling each other stories that weren't even really stories, just crumb trails of memory that we'd follow and follow until—

"Remember how we used to—" she said, swinging a leg over me in the astonishingly complete dark.

"Like this?" I said, grabbing her, and she laughed and yelped, louder than she would have let herself in the city. We were (how many times does a person get to say this, without qualification?) happy.

•   •   •

The first time Hannah was woken up by voices was at the end of September. We'd been there for a month—it felt already like we'd been there for a year—and the museum had just had its Fall Harvest Festival. This was one of the museum's biggest annual draws: kids digging up potatoes with dirty spades; apple cider in Dixie cups; churning butter with a crank. Hannah had convinced me to play guitar for it, so I'd sat on the stone wall in a period jacket, playing progressions I meant to sound vaguely autumnal, nodding at the families who stood and watched. The seasons were much more palpable in Hibernia than in the city—you could feel fall coming like a battle the whole town was getting ready to wage—but it was still warm enough most nights that we were eating dinner on the porch, sleeping with our windows cracked.

That night we ate barbecued chicken with crispy slices of potato that were more blackened than I'd meant them to be (I'd become a maniac for grilling on the little Weber I'd found out in the garden shed). At some point in those weeks we'd started talking concretely about our wedding, and this had prompted, or coincided with, the flickering of our period of late-summer bliss. What did I think of this venue's website? (Pictures of people drinking cocktails on an outdoor patio, a wedding tent set beside an apple orchard.) What were my feelings, generally, about rehearsal dinners? How important was it to me that all our friends be able to stay in one place?

I answered these questions with a sort of willed attention, a half distraction, and Hannah could sense it; the jokiness drained slowly out of our conversations.

It wasn't that we were back to the bickering and bitterness of the spring—we were still glad to have moved, and glad to be with each other. But something chillier had crept in. The museum was slightly less novel than it had been—Hannah was dealing with her first budget, the water softener needed to be replaced—and there is, I think, a special gloom that comes with wedding planning. It may just be the realization that the traps you watched swallow up a thousand people before you are going to swallow you up too. You sit down meaning to compose a love song, and you end up scheduling a conference call with a tent rental company.

"What if everybody camped?" Hannah said as we lay in bed that night.

"We'd have to rent the equipment, plus, the old people . . ."

"Yeah."

We finally fell asleep, and we'd been asleep for a couple of hours—long enough for there to be a cold spot of drool in the corner of my mouth—when Hannah bolted awake and asked if I heard people talking. The bedside clock said it was just past two in the morning. It was so dark in our room that I couldn't see her face. I lay my hand between her shoulder blades and listened, waiting for the coherent parts of me to untangle themselves. Maybe she'd been having a dream that we were still talking about the wedding. Maybe I'd been having a dream that she'd said anything at all.

"Listen," she said.

"I don't hear anything."

"Listen," she said again. "You don't hear people whispering?"

"Who would be whispering?"

She sighed and said, in a tone more of exasperation than fear,

"Can you go check?" So, with more grumbling than necessary, I swung myself out of bed and, trying not to bash my shin on the high first stair, made my way out into the museum. This was the first time I'd gone out into the museum in the middle of the night and I was surprised, walking barefoot through the kitchen exhibit and the living room, flicking on wall sconces as I went, to find myself not entirely at ease. The black windows. The rocking chair like a crouching animal. I understood, in a way I hadn't quite before, why little kids sometimes refused to set foot inside, what a basic thing fear is.

To be clear: I still didn't hear any voices. But you never quite hear *nothing* when you're in an old house in the middle of the night. The stairs to the second floor creaked as I made my way up. The windows rattled in their frames. One by one I looked in the rooms along the hallway: nothing in Edmund and Sarah's bedroom, nothing in the kids' bedroom, nothing in the study, nothing in the storage room.

Maybe it was mice that Hannah had heard; maybe it was a raccoon in the attic. Or maybe, most likely, it was nothing. I went back down to our room—willing myself not to rush—and climbed back into bed. My skin against Hannah's felt as cold as clay.

"Well?"

"There was nothing."

"We should get the alarm fixed," she said.

"I'll deal with it tomorrow."

The next morning, with the sun light-sabering around the curtains into our room, Hannah rolled over and said she was feeling sick. She was going to stay in bed, she said. Tell Donna to take over the museum. So maybe that's what happened last night, I thought. She'd had an actual fever dream.

Donna taught the class of third graders who came in at ten o'clock, and I helped. The kids sat clustered on the floor in the living room while Donna explained about Wright's encyclopedias; I wove through the group passing out worksheets and pencils. One blister-lipped boy in a stained turtleneck said please could I take him to the bathroom, *please,* then held my hand with his grubby little palm the whole way. Next to him on the floor there was a blond girl with a face from a Renaissance painting, cross-legged, carefully writing the cursive loops of her name across the top of her worksheet. Lifelong fates determined at age seven.

Even if Hannah hadn't been sick, I might have been helping out like this. I was spending more and more time working around the museum—which is to say less and less time writing music. My first few weeks I'd been sticking to a schedule, going up each morning to the empty exhibit room on the second floor with my guitar and my digital recorder, filling my little Moleskine with scraps of lyrics and semi-legible notations. Fishing for melody bits, which I'd then furnish with chords and choruses, the whole usual cycle of pleasure and desperation and drudgery.

I'd managed to finish a couple of songs this way, and I'd recorded them on my laptop, each one in just a few takes, only a couple of guitars per track. I'd gotten to where I could see how in a certain number of months I might have an album—it would start with ten or fifteen seconds of the sound of wind against the shutters—but then, just when I ought to have been feeling hopeful and energized, something had happened. I couldn't quite explain it—it was a feeling like being in a plane on the tarmac, gaining speed and gaining speed and then, just at the point when the wheels are about to rise up from the pavement, that terrifying miracle, the plane slows back down and becomes just a vehicle again. Joy is hard to sustain outside of relationships too.

Anyway, I didn't tell Hannah any of this—I hardly told

myself any of this. I just left my guitar on its stand and made myself more and more useful in the museum. There was never a shortage of things to do. Butch needed help replacing the deer fence around the garden plot. Donna needed help swapping out the signs in the kitchen exhibit. It's alarming how little meaningful work a person can accomplish while appearing busy.

I finished up with the class of third graders—they each got to take home a little satchel of herbs from the garden—and started cleaning up the bits of string they'd left in the grass. "Did you see when that short kid found a dead squirrel over by the bench?" Donna said. "I thought the teacher was going to pass out."

"I'll tell Butch to move it," I said.

Hannah, when I went in to check on her, was still in bed, pale and damp-skinned but awake. Strands of hair were plastered to her forehead. Something about the way she sat—slightly propped up, looking at nothing in particular, her hair loose over her shoulders—made me think of an old dying person in a movie, a nightgown and a sleeping cap.

"Are you okay?"

"I think so."

"Do you want some ginger ale?"

She shook her head. I lay the back of my hand against her forehead—only a gesture, since I never knew exactly how a forehead was supposed to feel—and told her I'd take care of the museum for the rest of the afternoon. Just before I left she said, "Wait. Will you hand me my notebook?" Her speckle-covered notebook was more and more like a sick person itself, worn and damp. She thanked me semi-audibly.

Hannah was one of those people who, when they get sick, bring almost a spiritual aspect to it. Teeth chattering, voice feeble, curtains drawn—she suffered like someone going through a biblical ordeal. Once, when we were still in Queens, she'd gotten the flu and spent three days subsisting on crushed ice and Carr's crackers, only opening her eyes long enough to let me tip NyQuil into her mouth.

Out in the museum there was an unusual amount of hubbub. Donna and Butch were unfolding a table in the living room, and there were chairs stacked next to the window. I'd forgotten that this afternoon was the monthly meeting of the Wright Society; the last one had been just a couple of days after we moved in. The society—they called themselves "the Wrighters"—consisted of three men and a woman, all from Hibernia or one of the couple of towns nearby. They sat around in the living room for an afternoon each month and talked about one of Wright's books, or about a period of his life.

Hannah's job was to provide them with a plate of Ritz crackers and apple slices, and to remind them about any upcoming evening programs; they'd loved Jim, Hannah's predecessor, but they'd happily taken to her, too. They were, in the way of most people who gather in the middle of the afternoon to talk about books by long-dead people, slightly crazy. My plan was to sit with them for ten or fifteen minutes, just long enough to be polite, before pretending to remember work that needed attending to elsewhere.

Today's topic was the unproductive last couple of years of Wright's life, what the Wrighters called "the Crisis." This was apparently a pet obsession of theirs—that Edmund had, toward the end of his life, stopped writing not because he was sick, or because he'd run out of ideas, but because he'd encountered something in the course of his work on spiritualism that had broken him like an egg. This whole topic was, I gathered, for them something like the JFK assassination—a mystery irresistible precisely because of the impossibility of their ever definitively proving anything.

"The problem," the woman in the group explained to me,

getting settled in her chair, "is that his spirit work was so spottily recorded, it's hard to know what he was doing even *before* he went silent. And this was a man who wrote down every thought. This was a man who wrote down how many bites it took him to finish his chicken."

"They'd just as soon we talk about something else, of course," said the wispy-bearded man who spoke in a not-quite-British accent. He made a face that managed to convey both disgust with the powers that be—Donna, I presumed—and resignation.

The leader of the Wrighters—a collapsing barrel of a man named Barry—wiped his mouth and said, "I'd like to put forth the notion that what happened was that he had a vision of William's death and he couldn't bear it, because if you look at what he was working on just before the April second letter—"

"But we don't *know* what he was working on," said the man who looked like a dissolute Viking, "because we haven't disproven the fact that Sarah buried him with an entire notebook, or multiple notebooks, and that's why to me this whole—"

"Oh, for God's sake. You and your burying. We also haven't disproven the fact that—"

The woman in the group, leisurely eating a grape, said, "Can we just take a second to say how sad it is, though? Can we? Here's this guy who'd written his way through so many problems, so many years, and all of a sudden he's just silent."

"But that's exactly my point! Maybe he *wasn't* silent."

They went on like this for an hour, bickering, laughing, pulling out and consulting their falling-apart copies of Wright's books, refilling each other's cups of seltzer. I stayed sitting with them for much longer than I'd meant to. They were retired schoolteachers and quilters and amateur genealogists, the sorts of people you see in library bathrooms—the Viking's pants, I noticed, were halfway unzipped—and they were as happy as if they'd been sitting around the table with Charlie Rose.

When they finally finished for the day, they all filed out of the house, calling, "See you in October!" and "I'm going to send you that article!"

Barry stopped by the door and turned toward me with an expression like he was considering asking me on a date. He had skin tags on his eyelids, and teeth like worn pebbles. "You and Hannah aren't letting Donna get to you with all her True Wright Legacy stuff, are you? That's what we were worried about, when Jim left. That she'd get somebody in here who just toed the company line, acted embarrassed about all the rest of it."

I could hear Donna gathering her stuff up in the exhibit room, getting ready to come downstairs.

"Nope," I said, with no actual notion of what he was talking about, "you'll never hear a bad word about Wright from us. We're big fans."

This seemed to do the trick. "Good, good, good," he said, tucking his books back into his backpack. "Tell Hannah to feel better. And see you next month."

Watching him walk out, I marveled, for the thousandth time since we'd been there, at the difference in people. This one walks around all day worrying about a song he's working on. This one can't stop thinking about whether she got her bulbs planted in time. This one cares only about the reputation of a stranger who died a hundred years before he was born.

"They clear out already?" Donna said. "You mind if I open a window in here?"

While I was folding the table and putting the chairs away, Butch came in carrying a big styrofoam cup and a plastic spoon.

"I was over at Peck's getting ant traps, and I bought Hannah some chicken soup."

"You didn't have to do that," I started to say, but Butch had that capacity that some people do to make any expression of gratitude, however mild, seem overwrought; he was the sort of shy person who would save your life in battle and then insist it must have been someone else.

Hannah ate the soup in bed, slowly, wincing at each sip. I perched next to her.

"I just didn't sleep at all last night," she said. The curtains were still drawn in our room, and the bed had the slight warm dampness of having had someone in it all day. Her notebook was on one side of her and a copy of Wright's selected letters was on the other.

Tending to Hannah always brought out the parent in me. Each time she moved to put down the spoon I made her take another bite. Finally she insisted she was done—she drew in her lips and twisted her head away; being sick brought out the kid in her—and so I slurped the rest.

"You'll get sick," she said.

"Eh."

"How was the school group?"

"Fine," I said. "Donna yelled at a boy who kept breaking people's pencils."

She nodded. "What about the Wrighters? Were they crazy?" Her eyes were closed again. Each word had to work slightly harder than usual to get out, a kind of swimming-up through thick water.

"Crazy as loons."

．　　．　　．

The next afternoon I was standing on the porch—having spent another day dealing with the museum instead of writing music—when I heard something from up by the porch's ceiling. A kind of rustle-chirp. There was a bird's nest there on top of one of the square wooden pillars that Hannah and I had been watching for a few weeks. She'd point it out to kids when they came in, and they would *ooh* and *ahh* and ask their parents to hold them up so they could see the eggs. And now, when I went over, there were six or seven baby birds in their place.

This was, I was fairly sure, just the thing to rouse Hannah from her sickness. She'd spent most of that day in bed too—she did have a fever, it turned out, and she'd had another bad night's sleep—but she'd gotten up that afternoon to take a shower, and the birds would nudge her a bit back further toward health. Life indomitable.

I called to her and she came slowly out onto the porch in the red robe that was illness incarnate. She rose up on her toes and peered into the nest, smiling feebly.

"Look at that," she said.

We'd never seen baby birds up close before, certainly none we'd known as eggs. They were these tiny waxy featherless finger-puppet-looking things, with beaks permanently open and pointing upward. "They're like aliens," she said.

"They're like velociraptors."

We stood looking at them, Hannah interested but maybe not quite inspired in the way I'd meant for her to be, until it was time for me to go in and clean up the quills and inkpots from that day's activity. The mother bird fluttered crabbily around our heads.

That night Hannah went straight back to bed after dinner, and just after I'd climbed into bed too—it couldn't have been any later than ten—it started raining as hard as I could ever remember it raining in my life. Just endless pounding and pounding, so loud that it woke Hannah up. I got out of bed and I couldn't even see outside—the windows were just squares of white. "Do you hear that?" I said, but she couldn't hear me. I imagined the house, the woods, the graveyard, the meadow, all being *Sorcerer's Apprentice*'d away.

But when I woke up the next morning—Hannah was already out of bed—the sun was out, the house was standing, and the world looked exactly as if it had never rained at all. "Are you better?" I called out. I was alone in our room. It was a cloudless bright fall day; the tree by our window didn't even look wet. I'd just turned on the coffee machine when I heard Hannah, out somewhere in the museum, say, "Oh no."

"What?" I called, figuring we'd missed the meter reader, or maybe a school group had canceled.

But she just said, "Oh no," again, so I walked out and found her standing on the porch with her hand over her mouth.

"What? Are you okay?"

She shook her head and pointed. The rain had washed the nest down from the rafters. The baby birds were lying on the floorboards, writhing, like tiny paraplegics tipped out of their wheelchairs. "Shit," I said.

"Why didn't we do something?" she said. She sounded borderline frantic. "It didn't occur to you when it was raining?"

"What could we have done?"

"We have to do something," she kept saying, leaning over them. "We have to do something."

"Are you sure you're okay?"

"I'm fine, I'm fine. *Do* something."

The plan we settled on was that I was going to scoop the birds up onto a shovel and then toss them, or place them, over in the woods by the side of the house, where nature would do its work. Which meant, we both understood, that they'd be eaten by snakes, or starve to death, or whatever horrible thing happened to half-dead baby birds; it just seemed more dignified, somehow, that they should do this in the woods—this was, after all, where the Wrights were buried—rather than on the museum's porch. Or maybe it was just that we wouldn't have to see them.

But as I approached them with the shovel from the shed— I'd also brought a flattened cardboard box to help in gathering them up—Hannah called out, "Stop! Stop!" Because the birds, or maybe just Hannah's unhappiness about the birds, had shifted into a more acute phase. They were struggling to move; when I leaned close I could hear that they were even faintly chirping. "Maybe we should leave them," she said. "Maybe they'll be okay." But none of them, in the time we stood watching, came even close to getting on their feet. A school group from Millbrook was coming in an hour, and the kids would have to step around this horror show just to get inside.

"Well, what do you want me to do?" I said, for the third or fourth time. I was in my boxers and T-shirt, holding the shovel, still barefoot.

Finally Hannah, in a voice so quiet I could hardly hear her, said, "I think we have to drown them. I don't know what else we can do."

I've thought since then about where this idea may have come from. There's an image, I think, from the collective folk wisdom fund, about taking an unwanted litter of kittens down to the pond in a sack—maybe this was a natural extension of that. Or maybe it was the rain that had given her the idea; the birds' trouble had started with water, so it might as well end with it.

Anyway, I didn't have a better idea, and I didn't want to argue. I went and got the metal trash can from the shed, lifted out the heavy bag of birdseed (there was, I saw but didn't tell Hannah, a long-dead mouse flattened at the bottom of the can), and then, using the hose next to the porch, I filled the can with a few inches of water. Wincing—my body, it turned out, was less okay with all this than the rest of me was—I swept the chirping, writhing birds, one by one, up onto the shovel, and then slid them down into the water. Each one was smaller than my pinkie. They all accepted what was happening to them, or at least they didn't have the energy or the musculature to resist. A couple of them plunged right under, a couple of others gasped at the surface for air, no more (or less) alarmed than they'd been on the porch. And so now I had to do a thing I very much wanted not to do, which was to press the ones that were still fighting for air under the water with the back of my shovel and hold them there.

Hannah had gone back into the museum by then, so I hoped she'd moved on to thinking about something else, but when I looked up I saw her stricken face in the window of the front hall. When all of the birds had stopped breathing (but not, horribly, stopped floating to the surface), I carried the can over to the edge of the woods and tipped it over, sending the birds and their soaked nest into the leaves, where they would, I told myself, make some beetle family's month.

I don't want to overdramatize—this was unpleasant, but it was also, to any actual rural person, to Butch, presumably no more noteworthy than emptying the mousetraps in the basement. I walked back inside, washed my hands, and went back to our room to put on pants.

But for the rest of the day, through that morning's school group and then the couple of visitors in the afternoon, Hannah wasn't herself. I felt it in the way she thanked me when I brought us back lunch from the deli on Cold Spring; I felt it in the set of her mouth while she was doing inventory on the computer after dinner.

That night was as clear and crisp as the night before had been rainy—the stars, when I stepped out into the backyard, looked like an enormous city seen from an airplane at night. "Come out here," I called, but she was in our room already and either couldn't hear me or had decided to ignore me. When I got into bed she was still treating me coldly—she held Wright's book of letters so it blocked most of her face—but just after I'd turned off my light and rolled onto my side to go to sleep, she took a breath and said, "That was so horrible."

We hadn't mentioned the birds since that morning. She sounded completely awake.

"I know," I said.

"I can't stop thinking about it."

"It's over," I said. "It's okay."

"But it must have been so awful," she said. "They were there for hours. And where was their mother? I didn't even think about it until later. Did you see her?" She was, I could hear, in danger of crying.

"What's going on?" I said, resting a hand on her hip. "Are you okay?"

"I am," she said. "I am. I'm just tired. I'm really tired. I'm okay."

We lay that way for a while, with my hand on her, but when I woke up an hour or so later, I could tell, from the feeling of her body or the rhythm of her breathing, that she was still awake. But I knew too (or anyway I told myself) that she wouldn't want me to say anything, that she wouldn't want me even to acknowledge that she wasn't asleep. Losing someone is not a trip along a straight road, but this—her fever, the birds—was a mile marker, and I blew past it. I rolled over onto my side away from her, the sheets wrapped around my arm, telling myself that I'd say something if she still seemed to be awake in ... I fell asleep again before I'd even finished the thought.

[from Lydia Gibbens's introduction to Edmund Wright, *The Encyclopedia of Ordinary Human Sensation,* volumes I and II, edited by Lydia Gibbens]

… What one must understand, in order to properly appreciate Edmund Wright's encyclopedias, is that in writing them, despite the seeming impersonality of the endeavor, Wright came the closest he ever would to penning an autobiography.

His ambition, in the encyclopedias, was as simple as it was quixotic. He would, with the precision of a scientist and the sensitivity of a man of letters, set down on paper all the suffering that a person could reasonably expect to experience in his life, and then all of the pleasure. And it was his hope that by comparing the two, he would once and for all settle the question that had haunted him since his earliest childhood. Though it may not have been his conscious intent, he was, with this pair of books, giving body to the conflict that had so bedeviled his parents' marriage, and so had formed the backdrop to his upbringing:

Was life, despite its myriad difficulties, an unfathomable wonder, as his pious and tenderhearted mother would have it? Or was it a Boschian array of horrors, punctuated only by inadequate bits of relief, as his revered but unstable father tended to believe?

Thus can these haphazard and incomplete lists be read as an account of the battle that raged first within the tempestuous marriage of Matthew Wright and Alice Riley, and then, long after they had passed away, within the ever-fertile mind of their eldest son. When Wright fled to Hibernia—hounded by creditors, beset with troubles—his plan was to complete and publish Volume I in the fall of 1868, and Volume II in the summer of 1869. They would, he wrote to his stable and successful younger brother Harry, "stand as the twin pillars at the center of my professional life." It will surprise no one familiar with Wright's biography that these plans were to prove unduly optimistic.

But the encyclopedias continued, until weeks before Wright's death, to function for him as a solace, a home to which he would return again and again between flights of curiosity—whether into spiritualism, or botany, or the science of anesthesia. In these books, never finished, the consummate intellectual dabbler found a subject—or rather a pair of subjects—that were finally beyond his powers to exhaust. Wright may have failed to settle the decades-old battle within himself, but he succeeded gloriously in illuminating the inner struggle, and the confounding blizzard of private sensation, in which modern readers—presented here for the first time with an edition worthy of Wright's original vision—may see their own lives reflected ...

[from Edmund Wright, *The Encyclopedia of Ordinary Human Sensation,* volume I: *Pains,* edited by Lydia Gibbens]

. . .

- Pain of central chest muscles, very nearly a sensation of fibers being torn, pursuant to certain especially violent acts of sneezing.

- Unbidden memories of one's deceased parents, very often colored with a vividness and intensity that outdoes one's daily sensory perceptions, and accompanied by feelings of remorse, longing for reunion, and a sense of matters never to be finished.

- Faint ache, quality of pulsation, just above one's eyebrows, quite as if one had, unconsciously, spent hours glowering with concentration.

- Tender sensation in right kneecap, most noticeable while walking out of doors; a component of this sensation's peculiar stamp being the irregularity of its comings and goings, viz. that it will manifest for a number of steps, intensifying almost to a quality of burning, before retreating quite as suddenly as it came, leaving its possessor in a state of anxious unease.

- Realization that said tender sensation is unlikely to improve of its own accord, and is in fact more likely to worsen and to act as a harbinger for pains both excruciating and various, afflicting body parts vastly more difficult to look beyond than the knees.

- Disappointment in oneself upon realizing that said tender sensation, despite consisting, in point of fact, of frankly negligible quantities of pain, has nonetheless darkened one's outlook considerably.

- The act of drinking water from a glass that has been left on a table for rather too long a time and has, in consequence, acquired a taste quite like the smell of an unswept corner of a room.

- The sensation of gazing into a mirror and finding oneself appalled, viz. realizing that were this face to appear before one on the street, one would without hesitation inwardly enumerate a great many flaws; this initial start very often being followed by the further, and equally dismaying, realization that only a certain wishful generosity of self-perception, even perhaps a state of delusion, has allowed one to look in a mirror all these many years without rendering a similarly severe series of judgments.

- The recognition that one is, according to all sensible scriptural and psychological definitions, vain.

- The rather debilitating sensitivity beside one's fingernail that results from the too-vigorous extraction of a hardened or pointed protrusion of skin.

· Quite the majority of dreams, viz. dreams of plummeting from a considerable height; dreams of finding oneself an object of fun; dreams of having regressed, either in chronology or in circumstance; dreams of having mislaid an object of tremendous import; dreams of being separated from a beloved person, frequently with associations of mortality or tremendous shame; dreams of conducting quite furious arguments, nearly always regarding matters that appear minuscule or frankly incomprehensible in the morning's light (and which tend nonetheless to color one's daytime relations with one's "dream combatant"); dreams of sexual congress with strange and unwelcome partners (which tend, similarly, to color one's waking interactions, lending commonplace interactions a quality of nearly intolerable embarrassment).

· The sudden dread that overcomes one in the wake of certain dreams, particularly those that are, for reasons of psychic self-protection or circumstance, interrupted prematurely, and the consequent sensation of having glimpsed, through a doorway ordinarily shut (and beginning already to shut again!), a thing both terrible and true.

. . .

4

The story we were told about Hannah's predecessor, Jim—to the extent we were ever really told one—was that he'd left because of a personal crisis. He'd been director for four years, beloved by the Wrighters, tense somehow with Donna and the museum's board, and then something had happened in his personal life—a breakup, maybe; a sudden illness—and he'd gone back to Poughkeepsie, where last anyone heard he was volunteering at a children's museum. Donna occasionally alluded to disagreements they'd had—Jim had wanted to do an exhibit on Wright's interest in water cures, which Donna thought was ridiculous—but all in all his name came up strikingly little.

We'd seen a picture of him—it was still on the Special Events page of the Wright House website (which looked like it was, and may in fact have been, designed on GeoCities). He was wearing a too-big beige blazer, posing with his arm flung around a startled-looking woman in purple. He looked like a long-serving, not-especially-beloved high school history teacher: a thin gray beard; a corduroy shirt that was probably missing buttons; a crooked smile.

The only time Hannah or I ever referred to him was when we heard something in the house, the walls moaning in the wind, a thump upstairs. This was, although I can't quite remember how it started, one of the jokes we had, that he was plotting to get back into the museum, maybe hiding out in the basement. "Jim's pissed tonight," I'd say. "I think he wants his Pert Plus back." Hannah once left a chocolate chip cookie on the mantel as an offering to him, the way you do for Santa Claus. That's what I expected him to stay for us—a private joke, a name on a stack of business cards in a drawer.

But that October, as it started to actually get cold, Hannah's fragility—her remoteness, her weepiness, whatever it was—got worse, and her capacity to make or appreciate jokes basically disappeared. She went from sleeping poorly to, many nights, sleeping hardly at all. Some of this, I figured, had to do with the museum: visitorship had declined from minimal to near nothing; an evening reading event that she worked on for weeks was attended by just me and Donna. And some of it may just have been seasonal, the general unnervingness of fall in the country. The line between romantic getaway and lonely creepy farmhouse is, it turns out, fairly thin. The yard and woods around the museum were carpeted in curled brown leaves. The windowsills were scattered with dry, dead flies. Driving back to the house from the grocery store, we wouldn't pass a single other car; if it weren't for the smell of fires burning in fireplaces, we might have thought everyone in town had been raptured away.

Hannah had stopped waking me up when she heard things at night, but as often as not now, at some point after midnight I'd hear her stand up and leave our room. This would always be in the absolute dark, when I was thickly asleep, so I would only register it blurrily; sometimes I wouldn't notice that she'd left at all until I reached over and found her side of the bed empty. In the morning she'd be back, and when I'd ask her how long she'd been up she would just make a noise that meant she didn't know, then roll over to get a few minutes of sleep before the museum opened.

Lack of sleep seemed not to be affecting her quite how I would have expected. She was shaky, preoccupied, but she was energetic, too, in an unsteady way. She came to me one afternoon—after weeks in which we'd hardly mentioned our wedding—with a heavily underlined ten-page printout about catering options, then the next day she told me to disregard it, that she was working on another. On the occasions when visitors did come into the museum, her tours went longer than I'd ever heard them. I'd hear her voice through the floor: "It's crazy, right? The weird thing—maybe Donna already told you—is that we don't even know if he ever meant to put them in any kind of order. He may just have wanted it to be jumbled up like this. Did you already see his study?"

She'd started exercising, too. Dislike of the gym had always been one of our bonds (for her this meant a pleasant softness around the hips; for me it meant wheezing at the tops of stairs), but now she was running each morning, out along Culver or on the little trampled path by the river, starting to get the prominent-collarbone look of the scarily fit. It was to try to help her sleep, she said. It was to give her an appetite.

I walked back across the fields behind the museum one Saturday after breakfast and she was sitting on the riverbank in her gym clothes, her headphones in her lap, looking out at the water, sweating. "Are you okay?" I said.

"I just saw a heron," she said, not looking at me. "He was up on that branch and then he just sort of dropped down and *whoosh*. I was going to take the canoe and see if I could find him."

At the museum the amount of work she did seemed to be in inverse proportion to the number of visitors we had: she wanted to form a partnership with the library; she wanted to plan a textiles exhibit. She was constantly in her little office under the stairs, scribbling in her notebook.

One afternoon Hannah came down from upstairs carrying an old cardboard Staples box. Donna, who'd been sitting reading at the welcome desk, leapt up. "Where'd you find that?" she said.

"I thought he would have taken it with him. Careful, I wouldn't be surprised if you find old tuna fish in there—the guy was a first-class slob."

Hannah walked right past her.

The box, which had belonged to Jim, was spilling over. Hannah had found it in the back of the storage closet. She carried it into our room, where she dropped it in the middle of the rug with a dusty thump. There wasn't tuna fish, but there were, piled in no discernible order, years of printed-out email correspondence; receipts from paint purchases made at Williams Lumber in 2008; flyers for the 2009 Spring Harvest Festival; notes on a lecture someone had given at the Rhinebeck Historical Society about nineteenth-century surgical practices; minutes from museum board meetings.

"You found his miscellany drawer?" I said.

"I think I found his brain."

She spent the rest of the night sorting through it, covering one edge of the rug in our room with little stacks of paper, organized by subject.

"Look," she said, holding up a piece of notebook paper covered in a drawing. I was at the sink, cleaning up after a spaghetti dinner of which Hannah had taken five bites.

The drawing looked like what a medieval person might have made of the solar system. Concentric circles, dotted lines, scribbled labels. In one corner there was a dark patch where someone had written something and then blacked it out. Across the top there was an 845 phone number in faded pencil.

"What could this possibly be?" she said. It was the happiest I'd heard her sound in weeks.

"Maybe he doodled when he was on the phone," I said.

"Here's another," she said, unfolding a paper with a smaller, equally incoherent drawing.

The next day the papers were packed up, the box back in the storage room.

That, apparently, was where Hannah was spending most of the time when she couldn't sleep. Organizing, she said. Reading old papers—of the museum's, of Wright's. Going through the collection. Thinking through how she could change the museum's marketing.

The storage room was, with the possible exception of the basement, the room in the house that I liked to go into least. It had been a baby's room once, apparently, tiny and yellow, with bowing walls, a slanted ceiling, and so many notebooks and binders and banker's boxes that you could only make your way into it sideways. And it wasn't only papers in there: there were tools, broken mops, a bike tire, a taped-together bundle of what looked like banister rails. Hannah had wedged a little red cushion against the wall on the floor, to sit on. The windows were covered with some sort of velum-ish material, to keep light from damaging anything. I imagined her up there like an ant in its chamber, piling and rearranging, piling and rearranging.

"Do you want me to help you?" I asked her one night. "You could read out loud and I could transcribe. It would go faster."

"No, I'm not going to make you do that," she said. "No reason for both of us to be up."

That night or the next one, I happened to wake up when the clock said it was 3:14 in the morning. Hannah wasn't in bed next to me. I decided—with the same sort of half-conscious lurch as when you decide to get up and pee—that I was going to go up and check on her. I wasn't—I really wasn't—trying to sneak up on her, but I was aware, as I climbed the narrow stairs, that I was setting my feet down carefully. The hallway upstairs was dark, but there was a light coming from the half-open storage room door. There's a way to walk across a creaky floor—just pressing with the edges of your feet—such that it doesn't make a sound; I wouldn't have guessed I knew how to do it. Without saying a word, without pushing the door any farther open, I moved my head to look inside and—Hannah was on her cushion, on the floor, reading something in her notebook. She clapped it shut.

"You're spying on me?"

"I wanted to see what you were doing up here."

She was standing up now, the notebook pinned under her arm. "Well, I'm reading. Congratulations. Go to bed."

"Why are you—"

"Just go to bed. I'll be down in a little." She sounded annoyed with me but something else too—embarrassed, scared, a little apologetic. Couples should carry dry-erase boards for writing messages to each other; their voices convey too much.

I did go back to bed, and a few nights later I was in the bathroom, rifling through the shelves in search of my tooth guard, when I came across her pill bottle. "Hannah Rampe. Risperdal, 1 mg. Take one pill every twenty-four hours, with water." The bottle was full, heavy as a roll of dimes. The refill date was September 24th, and it was now October 25th. My body reacted to this discovery faster than my mind; a cold current ran down my legs. I knew, of course, that Hannah took medicine, I'd watched her place the little white pills on her tongue, I'd witnessed the weekly filling and snapping of her pill case more times than I could count. But I only realized now how long it had been since I'd last seen her take one. Her weekly pill case, on the shelf below, was empty. Maybe this was just a backup bottle, and she had her real one in the bedroom. Maybe she'd been taking them on a different schedule lately because of her trouble sleeping.

I walked into our room holding up the bottle. I knew I needed to get this moment right—not a dad confronting his daughter with her stash of pot, not a husband catching his wife in a lie. Just a man wanting to get something straightened out. A minor confusion. She was kneeling by the radiator, adjusting the valve, and as she turned around I watched her expression change from a smile into a defensive scowl.

"Are you still taking these?"

Her doctor, she said, had switched her onto something else. It wasn't my business when. Since when did I monitor her medical treatment? No, I couldn't see the new bottle. Was I serious?

When Hannah lied there was a thing she did immediately afterward with her face and voice, a kind of snapping shut. Then she'd always move on, with unnatural speed, to some neutral, innocuous subject that had supposedly just come into her mind. This time she asked me if I'd remembered to turn off the lights in the exhibit cases upstairs. I didn't fight, I didn't press; I told her I hadn't and so I trudged upstairs, feeling somehow both as if I'd caught someone at something and been caught at something myself. I switched off the lights before coming back to bed.

Those next few days Hannah treated me with a deliberate, almost apologetic gentleness. She showed me a new set of places she'd been thinking about for the reception. At dinner she made a point of finishing her slice of the undercooked apple pie I'd made (Donna had gone apple picking a week before and now we had apples piled on every surface in our room, enough to feed all of Hibernia). She seemed so mild and normal that I decided I'd probably been wrong; she really was on a new medicine and she'd just for whatever reason been embarrassed to tell me about it. Maybe the only actual thing the matter was that she was engaged to someone who treated her like the subject of a police investigation.

We were standing out in the woods by the Wrights' gravestones when Hannah burst into tears and told me that she'd been lying.

This was at five o'clock on a Friday, just after the museum had closed after another day without visitors. We'd come outside to hang paper decorations in the trees—the house's Spooky Halloween Festival was that weekend—and to see if Edmund and Sarah's graves were in good enough shape for kids to do crayon rubbings. The sun was slipping down between the trees, and I was crouched in front of Edmund's grave, trying to hold the piece of tracing paper still. Hannah's wail was so sudden that at first I thought something had bitten her.

"I lied to you," she said, "I lied to you, I'm so sorry, I haven't been taking anything, something's wrong with me—"

I rushed to her—a jumble of crayons and cardboard ghosts and pieces of tracing paper fell out of her hands as she started to silently weep—and, not knowing what else to do, I put my hands on her shoulders and started in on the useless, automatic script: *What's going on? Are you okay? Everything's fine, what's happening? Don't worry.* I felt, all through my body, a kind of microscopic expansion, like a million little antennae raising.

The first thing she said once she'd gotten so she could speak again—by then I'd ushered her back to the museum, and we were sitting side by side on the front porch—was, "What if I'm not okay?"

"You are okay," I said. "You just need to be taking your medicine. We're going to go inside and I'm going to call Dr. Blythe." (Dr. Blythe, the therapist from her postcollege breakdown, was not a name I'd ever spoken before.)

"What if we get married and you're stuck taking care of a crazy person for the rest of your life?" she said. "What if I'm Mary Todd Lincoln? I would ruin your life."

"I've always seen a little of myself in old Abe."

She snuffled a laugh through her dripping nose, then started to cry again.

"Do you hate me for lying to you?"

"No. I'll hate you if you don't take better care of yourself."

"This hasn't happened before," she said. "I'm not sleeping, and when I do I'm having the weirdest dreams."

"What kind of dreams?"

But she just lowered her head onto her knees and turned her face away from me; from the shuddering of her back, I could feel that she was still crying.

After what felt like fifteen minutes—long enough that the sun had set completely, and there were goosebumps on our arms—she sat back up and said, "Are we going to be okay?"

"We're going to be fine," I said. "We're going to go inside and call Dr. Blythe, I'm going to make us dinner while you take a shower, then we're both going to get in bed and get a good night's sleep."

But that wasn't what she meant.

"Are we going to have a happy life?" she said.

"Of course we are. What are you talking about? We're going to have a great life. We already are."

She nodded quickly, trying not to cry again.

"Don't tell my parents about this, okay? I don't want them to be scared. Promise." I nodded, and then I watched her face break. "They should be nicer to you," she said. "They should be happier for us."

"It's okay," I said. "They will be. They'll be just fine. Let's go inside and call your doctor. Let's stand up."

"Let me call, okay? Let me call." Helping her inside reminded me strangely of the nights—there had only ever been a handful in our relationship—when she'd had too much to drink and I'd had to steer her into our bedroom, lower her onto the bed, help her off with her shoes and tights.

Once she was in her office chair, phone in hand, I stepped out into the hall and closed the door. Her office was just a little room underneath the stairs, and that moment, standing alone on the other side of the door, feeling my pulse synced up with the tick of the grandfather clock, is, for whatever reason, one of the sharpest memories I have of this entire period. Studying the cracks in the paint on the door, standing so my feet lined up entirely within the floorboard. I had the feeling (and this was very likely delayed shock from our conversation) that we were acting out roles somehow, that the house was a set and that there was an invisible audience somewhere that was watching both me standing waiting and Hannah in her office; I could feel them holding their breath.

Now I heard Hannah's muffled voice leaving a message for Dr. Blythe—I could only get the tone, which was ordinary, cheerful, apologetic, not the least bit weepy, as if she were calling to let him know about a scheduling mix-up. When she finally stepped out into the hall her eyes were dry and she was making the same sheepish face she did sometimes after fights. "Look at you standing there all freaked out," she said. "I'm fine." She took my hand and led us back out into the yard, to gather the decorations we'd dropped. It was hard to find the crayons in all the leaves. It had gotten even colder out. "Thank you for taking care of me," she said. "I'll be fine."

[Comment cards, Wright Historic House]

Ana Magloire—Poughkeepsie, NY

*Very informative museum, keep up the good work, interesting ency-
clopedias, the garden space is nice.*

David and Judy Diamant—Keene, NH

*Stumbled on this gem while visiting sister (Alice Sussler), free
afternoon. Wish there had been a bit more detail regarding food and
cooking, as have great interest and expertise in food of the period
and would be glad to return to make a presentation, including pre-
paring authentic recipes, if your schedule and budget permitted it
(whatachef@whatachefcatering.com).*

Raymond Farkas—Pine Plains, NY

*It has been years since I have had the privilege of visiting this fine
little museum, despite the proximity, as life does intrude (2 back
surgeries, 1 valve replacement, severe Lyme disease). Count me
among the "huzzahs" that you have not given in to those who
would prefer to see you closed. I am a veteran of the US Air Force
('51–'55, Bronze Star) and I understand that history is complex
and that sharing one man's story is a worthy and noble mission.*

Brian Gumley (age 7)—Hibernia, NY

The graves.

. . .

Spring 2020—New York—Age 39

You are sitting in a glass cube the air is damp it smells like bleach other moms sit next to you in red chairs they cross their legs open their bags you look out into the pool your son's swim class is in lane three you can hardly tell him from the others little hairless bodies big heads in red caps blue kickboards every sound splash whistle turned blurry at the edges your sandal hangs your knees look old you didn't know knees could look old the grout between the tiles is yellow the flyer on the wall says family swim on Saturday all ages welcome the mother next to you whose name you've never learned black hair is what you call her she says people keep telling us Corian that's supposed to be just like marble but you can actually spill on it which oh my god can you imagine me telling Simon he's not allowed to spill the back of your head hurts it's hurt all afternoon strange you're only realizing this now how many afternoons have you done this how many hours have you sat in this chair watched your son watched the clock above the lifeguard's chair you ask black hair do you have Tylenol you realize from her face that she was saying something you hope it wasn't important she looks into her bag she says I've only got these is that okay you say yes you say thanks that's fine . . .

5

There's an impulse, I've noticed, once someone's gone, to comb through your memory for moments—the more recent the better—when that person last seemed perfectly normal. *I just had dinner with him last week. I just got an email from her the other day.* Part awe, I think, and part protest: but she was *just* here.

Those next few weeks were full of these moments. The Halloween event, when Hannah wore her white sweater and knelt by the picnic table on the lawn helping the red-haired boy who'd spilled apple cider on his tracing paper. The afternoon when she stood talking in the entryway with the moldy-smelling man from Millbrook who was working on an article about defunct train lines. The morning when she was brushing her teeth and called for me to come quick (I can still hear her tooth-brushing voice, stretched out, all vowels), and there was a hawk standing watch on top of the locust tree.

Hannah had told me, at various points in those weeks, how much better she felt now that she was taking her medicine again. She'd made an appointment to see Dr. Blythe when we went back to the city for Thanksgiving. Sometimes, for no good reason, the internet just goes out—this was how I decided to think about what had happened to Hannah that October. The wedding, the move, the museum, her medicine—who knew how it was all interacting? In every system of sufficient complexity there are periods of inexplicable, and usually meaningless, disruption.

The night it happened I fell asleep before Hannah did—I was twenty pages into a history of jazz my dad had given me, and each paragraph was like a stone barricade that my consciousness could just barely climb. Hannah stayed up for a while after me going through her notebook (I remember the relief of her light going off), and then some number of hours later, I woke up to find her fingers on the waistband of my boxers. This would happen occasionally, but not for a while, that we would wake up *into* the act of sex. There was often an odd, impersonal ravenousness to it, as if our sleeping selves had made a rendezvous and our bodies were just the underlings. Sometimes we'd sink back into sleep afterward without having exchanged a single ordinary word.

But this time Hannah was fully awake (the moon must have been close to full, because when she pressed her forehead against mine I could see her eyes), and I remember her seeming unusually deliberate, even as I was still half-asleep. We are, I remember thinking, back in business. I can't, or anyway I won't, deconstruct the precise mechanics, but there was an emphatic quality to her movements, as if her hips and hands, her entire body, were a stamp pressing down with special force against a slip of paper. "I love you," she said, and then when I answered with a grunt or a kiss, she said it again. "I *love* you."

Afterward I slept like I'd been drugged, and when I woke up the curtains were pale and Hannah's side of the bed was empty. Her notebook was gone from the bedside table. It was 8:34, late even for me. My plan for the morning had been to fix up a verse of the song I'd been working on (there was a mushy stretch passing through A minor that I thought I might be close to solving) and then to drive to the hardware store to get new lightbulbs for the basement. Hannah's T-shirt and underwear were crumpled on the floor at the foot of the bed; her bathrobe was draped over the back of the chair by the window where she usually sat and drank her coffee. I poured myself a bowl of Chex and walked with it out into the living room.

Usually, at nine o'clock, Hannah would be setting up the museum—setting baskets of corn husks on each of the tables; counting out paper plates and pipe cleaners. I expected, after last night, for there to be a slight tender sheepishness between us; I would put my hand on her shoulder and she'd smile, tell me to knock it off whether I was doing anything or not. But she wasn't in the living room, and she wasn't at her desk, and she wasn't on the porch, and she didn't respond when I called her name from the foot of the stairs. Maybe she'd gone to get milk (no, our car was still parked outside). Maybe she'd gone for a morning run (except here were her sneakers, still muddy from the day before).

Donna came in at nine thirty—I knew from her sigh as she opened the door that it wasn't Hannah—and she said, as soon as she was settled, "Where's the boss lady?" It was only when I heard myself say, "I'm not sure, actually" that it occurred to me that anything strange might be going on. I still wasn't worried, exactly—I expected Hannah to walk in at any minute—but the seed had been planted. I called her cell phone, since I couldn't find it in our room, but the line just rang; maybe she'd turned it to Silent.

At ten o'clock a class of fourth graders showed up at the museum. Donna led them through candle making. I went upstairs and opened each door, the whole time talking to myself (*"Oh Hannah, this is ver-y weird"*) in that singsongy way you do when you think someone might be hiding. Nothing, nothing, nothing.

Butch was at the back of the house doing something to the hinges of the screen door. "I'm not sure where Hannah is," I told him, in a voice that I meant to sound more curious than concerned.

"Maybe she took a walk in the woods?"

I put on my jacket and walked out across the backyard, the same path we always took. It was a bright, clear day, fall photo shoot weather. I could hear the class back inside the house, Donna's voice repeating something. I walked past the birch trees, left at the bird feeder, and onto the muddy path through the woods. The stillness was bizarre. There wasn't a chipmunk, not even a bird, just half-bare trees and the sound of my footsteps and the smell of decomposing leaves. When I came to the hill where Hannah and I had once eaten cheese sandwiches and clementines I stopped and called her name, feeling slightly embarrassed, then turned back toward the house.

Each thought I had started out as an absurdity—could she have been attacked by a bear? accidentally shot by a hunter?—but then the more panicky parts of me would get ahold of it: jaws against that neck, *her* neck; blood in the corner of her mouth. Imagination is shameless. Suddenly I was walking faster, and the hair on my arms was standing up.

Your girlfriend, your fiancée, has started the day by going somewhere. That's it, a woman who has safely navigated thirty years of mornings is continuing the streak. She'll be standing in front of the class with Donna when you get back to the museum, and she won't be able to believe, if you even bother to tell her, what thoughts you were having while she was gone.

But she wasn't in the living room. And Butch, who looked like he'd been waiting for me, said, "Nothing, huh? She ever go walking by the river, or down toward eighty-two?"

Fear, like laughter, is a social phenomenon.

I got in the car—Hannah's green jacket was still in the passenger seat, a brochure from the Dutchess County Fair was crumpled on the floor—and drove down Culver, about as slowly as a person running. Past the house with the corn crib, past the house with the "Repeal the Safe Act" sign, past the fallen barn.

I looked through woods, up people's driveways, over big empty fields. I thought about rolling down the window to call her name and realized that this was an impulse borrowed from looking for lost dogs. A young mother came jogging out of her driveway with a kid in a stroller and we exchanged waves as if I were heading to the post office.

Then the thought occurred to me: Hannah's parents. Maybe they'd come to pick her up. I imagined them driving up at dawn, having decided to make one last plea for her not to marry me. It made more sense than anything else I'd thought of. I pulled onto the grass by the side of the road to see if I had reception so I could call the Rampes. But what if she wasn't with them? What would I tell them then? The dashboard clock said it was 10:59.

Curiosities slide into idle fears slide into terrors without there being any clear points of demarcation. I think I still would have guessed, if forced to bet, that nothing serious had happened, that I'd forgotten an appointment she'd told me about or that she'd gone on a bizarrely long walk or that a neighbor had invited her over. The lifetime batting average of my worried mind was infinitesimal.

But back at the house the school kids and their bus were gone, and Donna and Butch were standing by the front window in the living room, looking concerned.

"Not to get into you-all's business," Donna said, "but you weren't having some kind of fight or anything? When I was little my mom used to sometimes take off for a whole day, let my dad just sweat it out."

Butch kept stepping out of the room and I realized he was making phone calls from Hannah's office. "Well," I heard him say, "it's just strange. Yep. Uh-huh. Appreciate it."

"Oh *yoo-hoo!*" Donna called out toward the back of the house. "Doesn't it feel like she's just maybe hiding in the basement or something?"

Butch came back in and said, "I just talked to Jeanne down at the farm stand. She'll keep an eye out." Then, a few minutes later, after another call, "That was my buddy Ed, over on Charwell. He hikes Culver Mountain most mornings, and he said he didn't see anybody."

So, a search party.

Each time the museum phone rang, I'd think for an idiotic instant that it was certain to be Hannah, but each time it would be some well-meaning neighbor with nothing to say. "Was she maybe doing something in one of the schools?" "And did you see her leave the house?" Sitting at the activity table felt like being in a hospital waiting room, except with the knowledge that what we were doing might turn out to be ridiculous.

A young woman with a tote bag walked in at twelve thirty— she was a senior at Bard, and she'd made an appointment the week before to speak with Hannah about volunteer opportunities. Donna took her around, showed her the study. I paced between our room and the activity room, putting off the moment of calling Hannah's parents, going over to the fridge every few minutes to eat a spoonful of peanut butter or a few bites of congealed oily pasta. I was as hungry as I'd ever been in my life.

I finally did call Hannah's mom. "Do you think we should drive up?" she said, sounding more confused than anything else, and when I told her no, it was probably nothing, she said, "I'm sure you're right. But do have her call us."

At one thirty the museum phone rang again, for the first time in an hour. I was by the front window, Butch was in Hannah's office. "Mm-hmm," I heard him say. "Mm-hmm. Yeah? Whereabouts? Okay." He hung up and walked out toward me.

Even now, it physically hurts to remember this. I once dislocated my shoulder playing football in Norwood Park and I remember as I was lying in the dust with Brendan Wexler standing over me, I thought, *There's something almost beautiful about how much this hurts.* The pain had sophisticated patterning, a distinctive shape, it was like an iceberg exploding in slow motion in my nervous system. Remembering that moment of Butch coming out of the office feels like that.

"That was Mary Klougher," he said. "Says she might have seen something a little ways down the river."

I speed-walked with Butch, neither of us talking. We walked back from the museum over the stony yellow hills and then down along the riverbank, five or ten minutes, which is plenty of time for me to have tortured myself with every possible thing that could have happened, but I can't remember what I actually thought about. Did I know already, at some depth? Was I terrified? Hopeful? Or was I so focused on getting there that the entire walk was just an adrenalized mindless blur, like a parent racing to grab a toddler out of the road?

Mary Klougher stood waiting for us between the back of her house and the river. I'd never seen her before. She had on jeans and a flannel shirt, and she had the long gray hair of someone who cares deeply about horses.

What she'd seen, it turned out, was a canoe washed up onshore. She pointed to it now; it was flipped over on its back, red and brown, unmistakably the museum's, buried enough in reeds that I might have missed it. The last time I'd seen it, it had been leaning against the tree where it always lived, and Hannah had made me come look at a spiderweb on one of the oars.

"I was just going for a walk, then I saw it, and I thought, 'cause I'd heard from Jeanne that somebody was missing, hey, that's a little weird."

My internal temperature had plummeted such that my teeth were now chattering.

"Hannah ever go out paddling?" Butch said.

I told him yes, a few times.

"Could also have been a kid or something pushed it out, though, right? You-all just kept it over in the woods somewhere?"

Yes, back farther upstream, I said, behind a tree.

There's something particularly awful about feeling terror on a sunny afternoon. Hawks were circling way overhead, the river was smooth and coffee-colored.

I walked the few feet down the riverbank and touched the water with my fingers—it was cold but not freezing. This is, I told myself, a river that nine-year-olds safely paddle down without getting their bologna sandwiches wet. This is a river that Hannah called a glorified creek.

I could actually hear my heartbeat.

I don't know if I'd ever experienced true, sustained panic before. I understood, now, why people might run back into burning buildings, or how people could forget, in moments of crisis, how to dial a phone. I don't think I could have added three and four right then. I'm not sure I could have told you my full name.

There is, of course, a shameful excitement to these kinds of scenes. Not for me, but for Mary Klougher, and for the neighbors who'd now wandered back out of their houses. They were buzzing, conferring, going inside to make phone calls. I'd felt it before myself, watching fire trucks swoop to a stop, witnessing a mugging. Their disaster, your adventure.

A stork-looking man came out from one of the stone houses—he was cleanly bald, frowning—and announced that he was going to get his kayak from his garage. Butch was standing in a patch of grass a few yards downriver, looking out toward the opposite shore. I heard Donna saying to someone, "Who would think about going canoeing in November, though?" I leaned against a boulder by the shore facing away from the river, wondering if there was any way I could make myself pass out and then be woken up once all this was over.

After some number of minutes the stork man came dragging his kayak across his yard, and then some number of minutes after that he came back from his exploratory paddle, clambering up the shore, his paddle on his shoulder. "Nothing doing that I saw," he said. "I went maybe five hundred yards up and back." I stood up to say something, but then I realized that I might actually be about to faint, which suddenly seemed not at all desirable. Butch put a hand on my shoulder and said why didn't we walk back up to the museum.

"We're gonna find her, buddy," Butch said.

"I know."

She'd been gone for at least seven and a half hours. My shoes were muddy and my hands were shaking; I made the decision right there on the crest of the hill: if she was okay, if she was at the museum, we were going to get married immediately. Forget invitations, forget caterers—we'd drive to the courthouse that afternoon, never out of each other's sight again.

No. She was nowhere inside. You can feel when a house is empty the same way you can feel when a TV is off. I walked back into our room. Her robe was still hanging over the back of her chair, her wallet was still on the dresser. Someone you love going missing is a tightening vise: each second of understanding that this has actually happened, and that any possible resolution is not going to be one you like, is another twist. "I'm going to call the sheriff," Butch said. That, I think, was when the vise twisted tight enough that something happened to my breathing, or to my brain: suddenly there was a high whining sound in my ears and an extra layer of distance between me and everything around me. I sat down in the chair by the welcome desk and pressed my fingertips against my eyelids.

"Since either late last night or early this morning," I half-heard Butch say. "She may have gone out on the river. Why don't you go ahead and send as many folks as you can spare."

．　　．　　．

The sheriff pulled into the museum's driveway in a car that actually said "SHERIFF" on the door. He had sunglasses hanging from his collar and a belly like the prow of a ship. Explaining to him and his two deputies what had happened forced me to get myself more or less together. "What you want," he said, pulling a backpack from his car, "is to try to find her before the sun goes down."

The next half hour was all cars pulling into the driveway and along the road, as if there were going to be a party. Don and Jeanne from the farm stand. Butch's wife and his twentysomething son, who looked just like Butch except thinner and with a crown-of-thorns tattoo on the back of his neck. The checkout woman from Peck's with the hairline smoking wrinkles all around her mouth. Barry, the head Wrighter. A handful of people I'd never seen before. I felt in serious danger of bursting into desperation-and-gratitude-induced tears.

Sheriff Cole divided us up into teams: he sent some of us back down to the river, some of us into the woods west of the house, some of us out along the road. He distributed walkie-talkies, one per group. He assigned me to the woods, along with a grandmotherly woman and a scoutmasterish goateed man. While we walked—dead wet leaves everywhere, bare tree trunks, coffee-bean clusters of deer poop—the scoutmaster kept stopping to whistle with both pinkies in his mouth, as loud a sound as I'd ever heard a person make. I felt a general gelatin-boned shakiness that I think must have been adrenaline poisoning. "This is going to turn out just fine," the grandmotherly woman told me. "My son once went missing for a full night, dinner to breakfast. I imagine Hannah might just have gone off for a walk by herself and not told anybody."

Every single rock, bird, half-rotten tree stump, seemed for a millisecond like it could be Hannah—crouching down to tie her shoe, standing behind a tree; I kept thinking I felt my cell phone buzz, which I didn't; there was no reception in the woods—but still, each time, my heart would leap and I'd tear my phone out of my pocket thinking I'd see "Hannah" on the screen and the whole nightmare would dissolve. The scoutmaster said I was looking a little gray and made me eat a few bites of a granola bar that he pulled out from one of his many pockets. I had a vision of him, for some reason, with a full emergency kit in the trunk of his car, leaping out to set up road flares around a minor accident. "You just finish that up," he said. "You want to hold on to something? You all right?"

Every fifteen or twenty minutes my panic-despair would be pierced by a voice saying that this was all insane, us tromping around the woods, splashing into the river, that I'd dragged half the county in to witness the breaking of an engagement. Because that, more and more, was how I thought this was going to end: her shamefaced reappearance, a weeping fight, a U-Haul. Maybe that emphatic middle-of-the-night sex had been her goodbye. Maybe she'd met someone else.

As soon as I had the thought it was like lock tumblers falling into place: of *course* she'd met someone. The sleeplessness, the shiftiness, the guilt. It was the only way any of it made sense. I felt a spike of such sharp relief, thinking of it, that I had to hold on to a tree. This wasn't a life disaster; this was a romantic disaster: she was walking teary-eyed by the side of the road, or (God help me) she was off fucking someone, in a motel or in a backseat, maybe the organic farmer with the Adam's apple, maybe one of the Wrighters, anyone, please, just please, let her be alive and not dead. I'd be furious, humiliated, devastated, but oh God I would collapse to my knees with gratitude, it would be the most wonderful day of my life.

I scrambled the half mile through the woods back up to the museum, my lungs burning, and called Hannah's phone again from the phone in her office. It rang and rang, and I heard each ring as an event with a beginning, a middle, and an end. *You've reached Hannah Rampe . . .* "Hannah, if you're getting this, I don't care what you're doing, I don't care who you're with, you need to call back, you need to call back right now, I'm completely freaked out, and—" I waited a minute and called again, in case she'd heard my message and had a change of heart. *You've reached Hannah Rampe . . .*

Back down in the woods, where my group was now walking up a rocky hill along a dry stony creek bed, the prospect of sunset (it was now five o'clock) had started giving an extra urgency to things. Sheriff Cole walkie-talkied everyone to say that we should regroup back at the museum if we hadn't found anything by six. There were, through the treetops, a couple of pale stars out already, there was wind rattling the few leaves still hanging on. Hannah and I would usually have been in our room with the radio on, maybe splitting a beer, deciding whether to drive to Peck's or just to cook with what we had.

There was now (there are terror cycles, just like there are sleep cycles) such a deadness in my limbs that I wasn't sure I could keep moving. I felt minutes away from collapsing into the leaves. There was no possible way I was going to be able to survive it, if searching for her went on all night, then all day tomorrow—but there was also no possible way it was going to end any sooner than that. The places she could be were so many; the places we could look were so few. I imagined Sheriff

Cole setting up a tent on the front yard with cots in it, like they have at disaster sites. We'd sleep in shifts. Maybe the Poughkeepsie police would loan us a helicopter. Hannah's face would be on the news. I'd spend the rest of my life stapling flyers to telephone poles, wandering median strips.

No. The group that found her was farther down the river than Sheriff Cole had told anyone to search, past the swimming hole where we'd skinny-dipped. The call came through at 5:50, just dark enough that the woods and air were starting to turn blue and smudged. The group had gone outside the walkie-talkies' range, so one of them, Butch's son, had had to run back a bit, which explained some of how his voice sounded when it came through. "We found her. We found her. We're about three hundred yards down the river." He didn't have to say whether she was okay; all of our faces fell together, as if a handful of strings had been snipped.

Without thinking about it, or even realizing that I was doing it, I ran back through the woods and across the fields and down the riverbank, hopping over brambles, climbing fallen trees, squelching through mud, nearly falling in. I was in incredible pain, all over my body, but my legs weren't heavy anymore, I could have leapt over a car. I was making a steady rumbly groan. When I finally came to Butch's son (his jeans and shirt were soaked, he'd been fully in the river, his neck was streaked with mud), I stopped, panting, trying to get out the words *Where is she?* and Sheriff Cole, who I hadn't noticed running beside me, stepped in front of me, to block my view. "Take a seat right here," he said, pushing me down onto a tree stump. He was shaking too, and panting. "You just wait right here. We'll get her." There were other people around me now, Donna and the scoutmaster and Jeanne from the farm stand, more people, all pressing on my shoulders, petting my head, squeezing my hands. Someone told me to close my eyes and I did. I heard, a little ways off, someone splashing out into the river, something like branches breaking, some kind of conversation, more splashing. That may have been when I started wailing, almost screaming, a sound I would never have recognized as coming from me; the hands were pressing harder against me now, and I thought, in the part of me that was still observing, like a guillotined head's blinking eyes: *This is the sound a person makes when he's burning alive.*

PART TWO

. . .

[Edmund Wright's journal]

Oct. 3

... The events of the night have left me troubled to my toes. Shortly after supper I retreated to my office for a final grapple with the morning's pages. I sat at my desk, just as I sit now, with my left elbow upon the table & my left temple upon my fist, just so. The moon hung in the window's corner; Sarah & her dishes clattered companionably below. As I became consumed in the rhythms of my work, I grew conscious, dimly, of a strange sound somewhere in the room behind me. A cursory look persuaded me that I had been subject to one of perception's manifold illusions, but in the ensuing quarter hour the sound, rather like breathing or distant chatter, persisted, & my bare animal sense, both more elusive & more reliable than hearing, insisted that there was indeed a presence in my study & that my very looking had been the cause of its earlier dissolution. Carefully, then, oh so carefully, I set down my pen & I made myself like a creature of prey in a meadow, still & abuzz with the readiness to perceive. Here the figure came, then, closer now, closer, seeming not so much to tread as to flow across the room; the flesh between my shoulder blades now fairly quivered. When the figure was, by my body's reckoning, close enough to reach my neck, the sound of its breathing, the very imprint of its presence, identified itself to my inmost apparatus & I leapt: it was William. Helpless now to restrain myself, I spun around in my chair & in so doing I scattered being & sensation both. I had evidently let

out a cry, for Sarah called my name from the foot of the stairs &
I replied, in tones of willful muscularity, that it had been nothing,
pardon me, that all was well. And so it seemed; my study showed
nothing uncommon & after some minutes I returned to my papers,
telling myself that I had received a dispatch not from my son but
from some ordinarily unreachable depths of my psyche, made acces-
sible by exhaustion. Yet the experience lingered, & lingers still,
rebuking me, imploring me to trust my senses & not my reason;
what a fool I would be if, out of fear & obstinate materialism, I
failed to redeem in the currency of understanding the profoundest
loss of my life. Thus does a man of science set down his tools &
become once more one for whom the world contains wonders both
terrible & incomprehensible. How fervently, waiting here once
more in the dark, do I both dread & long for William's return . . .

1

There's a moment, after you wake up from a nightmare, when you realize: *Wait, so I don't have to worry about* any *of that.* Those days right after Hannah died were the opposite of that, only over and over and over again. *It's true. It actually happened. This is now my life.*

I can't really say, now, whether I actually believed that Hannah's death had been an accident, or if this was just the workings of my psychological immune system trying to protect me from taking on too many agonizing thoughts at once. Anyway, I was too staggered, in the immediate aftermath, to do much coherent thinking. I was at my full capacity just trying to navigate a single block.

I came back to the city a day or so after she died, but I have no memory of how, or exactly when. I don't remember anything about being at the medical examiner's office, except that there was scented Kleenex in the waiting area and that I didn't look at the photo. I do remember going to the Rampes' apartment, though. This was a day or two before the funeral; the arrangements had all been made horrifyingly quickly. The Rampes' doorman, Dominic, who must have been letting up desperate-looking people in an uninterrupted stream for days, just nodded at me. The elevator looked unchanged, which was somehow both surprising and awful. The feeling at the Rampes', as soon as the door opened, was like a sick ward. There were unopened bundles of mail on the floor, used tissues and empty plates on every surface. Bruce was in gray sweatpants, unshaven, red-eyed, his own homeless doppelgänger. Terri was in a worn blue bathrobe, frantically edgy, not wearing any makeup. It was stuffy inside the apartment, but her whole body was shaking.

"She's gone!" she said, hugging me. "She's gone! My daughter is dead! *Dead!*" I had the feeling, somehow, that Terri was testing out the word, like striking an old-fashioned alarm bell, at first tentatively, then louder and louder, not quite believing that the horrible, epic occasion—the life-changing emergency—had arrived.

The reason the Rampes had summoned me—I don't know if they'd told me this or if I just understood it—was so I could officially debrief them on the day of Hannah's death. They'd heard the story from the medics, and from the medical examiner, and even, in a weeping incoherent phone call from Hibernia, from me, but they wanted more. Misery loves detail.

We sat in their living room, in the same chairs where we always sat, their dog, Mickey, asleep at Terri's feet. I remember feeling flayed inside, like every vein in my body had been scraped with a blade. I also remember having the surreally clear thought: *So it's actually true—none of this can protect you.* By which I meant, the doors that close smoothly, the walnut bookshelves, the speaker system designed by a patient of Bruce's who'd also done the sound for *Wicked.* There are no fortresses.

I did my best to walk them through the day she died, starting with the moment when I woke up in bed alone. I remember the looks on their faces—attentive, shattered—much better than I remember anything I said. Terri kept clawing at the arms of her chair, grimacing. When I'd gotten through most of it we sat there and wept together, freely and loudly, like a three-part chorus. Bruce's mother, Hannah's grandmother, who I hadn't known was in the apartment, and who lived alone in an Arizona condo, came tottering in from the kitchen looking hunched and sunbaked, cleared away some dishes, and didn't even look at me.

My decision not to mention anything about how Hannah had been doing before she'd disappeared—the Risperdal, the sleeplessness—didn't feel like lying. It felt—to the extent that anything I did in those days felt like more than the reflexes of a wounded animal—like prudence, like loyalty. I wasn't telling them about her meltdown in the same way that I wasn't telling them about our sex life; there are layers of detail that belong only to the people in a relationship.

And I knew what these details would have suggested to them. I didn't want them to even entertain the possibility that Hannah had killed herself—which, again, I didn't think she had. I didn't mean to be protecting them from the truth; I meant to be protecting them from a horrible misimpression.

"Who was the one who actually carried her away from the river?" Bruce asked.

"The police. The sheriff must have gone and got a stretcher from somewhere."

They both nodded, then Bruce clutched at his stomach and closed his eyes.

Whenever I thought we couldn't possibly cry anymore—we must have sat there for twenty minutes, all of our mugs of tea going cold—a wail would go up from Terri, and we'd start all over again.

"You loved her," Terri said at one point, between sobs.

"I did."

"And she loved you."

"She did."

"We loved her so much!"

If you listen to sobbing long enough, and if you're tired

enough, the sound breaks off from its meaning and becomes something else. One minute it sounds like an animal trying to throw up; then like someone shivering on an ice floe. At its most intense, it sounds—and this is somehow especially horrible— just like someone laughing hysterically.

. . .

I'd hoped to avoid going too much into my family, but I think I'd better tell you at least a bit about my parents. They came up to New York for the funeral—they installed me in a hotel on Lexington and sat by me while I shook and force-fed me spaghetti. For those few days, anyway, they were close to the center of my life again; for the first time since I was twelve, my family—the version I'd Magic Markered in kindergarten, lamented to the guidance counselor in middle school—was whole.

The condensed version of my parents' marriage is: they got married because they'd each been disappointed by someone else—my dad the daughter of his childhood piano teacher, my mom a young civil rights activist from Wesleyan—and then they spent the next twenty years learning that this was not a good reason to marry someone. They had me halfway through this process of discovery; my existence was the only enduring result of a decades-old folly, and probably the only thing that made them wait as long as they did to extricate themselves from it.

My dad, Robert Beron, was, like nine-tenths of the parents I knew in D.C., a lawyer. But he wasn't a box-seats-to-the-Redskins, deal-making, partners'-retreat type of lawyer—he made practicing law look as glamorous as selling vacuum cleaners. When he had me he was already in his forties. He was—is—a big disappointed leonine man, still with a full head of gray hair at seventy, dental work from another era. He was, I remember realizing at some point in elementary school, too old to really play sports with me. I'd see my friends' dads—boyish men racing around Father-Son games in sweaty T-shirts and running shoes—and feel a secret stab of shame for my dad, sitting on the sideline in his worn gray suit and broken shoes, doing paperwork in a too-low lawn chair. I always had the sense, sartorially, that he would have preferred to live in the era when men wore hats. And I think he would have had better luck in building a family in that era too—a wife who craved his praise, a son who aspired to drive a stick shift.

Instead he had my mom, Eileen, who was only a few years younger than he was but who could, culturally, have been his daughter. She was—is, is—an actual hippie, with long gray hair and clothes that involved large buttons and colorful scarves and skirts that looked like they'd spent months crushed in a drawer. She spent her entire career doing a job she didn't care about— she wrote policies in the National Labor Office of Blue Cross Blue Shield—and wishing she had the courage to go and illustrate children's books. This I think was the bewilderment at the heart of their marriage: why my mom couldn't be satisfied by the life she had, but couldn't be stirred to build the life she might have wanted. In my most durable childhood memories she's sitting in her chair in the den—a patched beige easy chair that was practically a living animal—with her library books stacked up around her like ramparts, her feet drawn up under a complicated assemblage of clothes and blankets. She didn't think she was cut out for motherhood—she used to tell me this semiregularly—but rather than try to do better, she would always just apologize, and encourage me to go into therapy.

I don't know what finally led to the divorce—one Thanksgiving my dad announced the decision as hurriedly as an embarrassed grace—but I remember that the house felt empty, and that I suddenly had much less trouble convincing my mom to buy me microphones and amps. I was in seventh grade. I had shaggy hair and a chain that ran between my wallet and my jeans. I painted my bedroom black; my mom redid all the house's bathrooms; my dad moved to a formica box of an apartment on L Street and never had milk in the fridge.

Both of my parents tried dating other people—my dad was even briefly engaged to a devoutly Presbyterian woman named Sally, who'd once worked for him—but by the time I left for college they'd both settled into not particularly agreeable solitudes. My dad developed an interest in World War II history and a chronic cough. My mom read Scandinavian mysteries and drove sandwiches around D.C. to housebound elders. I learned to divide my visits home as neatly as a diplomat. I learned to answer each one's questions about the other with vague misdirections. All this seemed perfectly natural. It was, eventually, the families without a divorce who seemed like outliers to me; I thought of them as freakish somehow, self-deluded.

But even in me, apparently, some *Parent Trap* strain of sentimental wishing had managed to survive all the way into adulthood. Because when my parents came to New York for Hannah's funeral, there was a moment—not a long one, but a moment—in which I just wanted them to scoop me up and cradle me, for the three of us to collapse into a king-sized bed and sob, a single warm mass. I actually had the thought: *If only we'd stayed together, then none of this would have happened.*

"Oh, Nick," my dad said, pressing me into his overcoat.

"You poor, poor thing," said my mom.

For most of their visit, though, I was too bewildered and miserable even to register their presence; I would just weep in bed or on the floor while one or the other of them called around to doctors to see if anyone would prescribe me Valium. Something they don't tell you about grief is how much it hurts, physically; I felt like someone had gone over me with a meat tenderizer. I remember at one point sitting up to read the first article that appeared about Hannah's death—not an obituary, just a three-line stub from the *Poughkeepsie Journal*—and then having to go lie down on the bathroom floor while my mom rubbed circles on my back. I remember eating three bites of scrambled eggs at the restaurant off the lobby and then having to be helped into the glass-and-gold elevator, my parents on either side of me as if I were an athlete with a broken leg.

Both of my parents had known Hannah, of course, but at a distance—they hadn't known her well enough to really grieve for her themselves. For Hannah's twenty-ninth birthday my mom had sent her a copy of *A Thousand Splendid Suns* with a "40% Off" sticker and a barely legible note ("I hope you haven't read this"). Whenever my dad and I talked on the phone—a monthly obligation—he would end the conversation by saying, "Tell Hannah hello." But they'd never really known what she was like; they hadn't known our life. They'd been spectators to the business of our wedding planning ("You aren't going to have us walking you down the aisle, are you?" my mom had asked), and they'd shown no inclination whatsoever to visit us upstate (though my dad had asked how near we were to Cooperstown). What comfort they could give me was mostly generic or accidental.

The night before the funeral the three of us were sitting around a table at the dark hotel bar, nibbling a bowl of cashews, watching people go back and forth from the lobby. My mom had started talking about an old neighbor of ours on Veazey Street, Marcia Popkin, who now had MS and was having to install a wheelchair ramp in her house. "I remember her husband just working out in that garden for *hours*," my mom said. "In that big gray shirt. I never walked by when he wasn't working."

"Do you remember how nasty she was when I dented their car?" my dad said. "Do you remember that? The tiniest dent. And what was their weird little daughter's name? The gymnast?"

I said I thought I remembered him denting their car and Eliza, the daughter's name was Eliza.

"Were they the ones with the dog whose hair all fell out?"

"That was the Hirschmans."

Occasionally, very occasionally, it would happen that the horror of Hannah's being gone would recede for a few minutes and I'd get a window of dreamy, flu-ish distance from everything—this stretch at the hotel bar happened to be one of those times.

"Isn't it astonishing?" my mom said, after a silence.

I understood that she didn't mean Marcia Popkin's MS, or the three of us being together, or even that my fiancée's funeral was in the morning. Or anyway I thought I understood. Because my thinking, in these periods, had the same strange refracted quality as when I was on the edge of sleep, that same mix of lucidity and incoherence. And right then, as my dad signaled for the check, it seemed to me that my mom must have been thinking what I was thinking: that *every* house is a haunted house. I'd been thinking a lot about the Wright Museum, of course, and how unbearable it would be if I ever set foot there again. But now I was thinking about the house I'd grown up in, where my mom still lived—three stories, pale blue, with the beige driveway and the taped-over doorbell—and I could see it surrounded by the ghosts of men working in their gardens and girls carrying gym bags and dogs going bald. And I could see us haunting it too, younger versions of ourselves trailing around with bags of microwaveable popcorn and broken plastic laundry baskets and—but I was too tired to finish the thought.

My parents were standing up; my mom had her hand on my shoulder.

"You should go to bed, sweetie."

"It's an early day tomorrow."

"Right."

Hannah's service was at the same enormous stone temple on Eighty-fourth Street where she and I had gone with her parents for Yom Kippur. I'd woken up with an iron-spike pain above my right eye, so I'd taken two Excedrin on top of the Valium that my mom had managed to procure for me. Men in black suits stood by the temple doors. The coat room off the lobby was as messy as a preschool cubby area. Hannah's Oberlin friends, a gaggle of food-co-op-looking people, came up and hugged me one by one. Most of them were crying already. A blond man named Felix, who seemed to know me, and who had a tattoo of a fish poking out from the sleeve of his jacket, told me he would never forget, absolutely never forget, what Hannah and I had done for him when he'd been having such a hard time with his sister. The only thing I could manage to say to anyone was "Thank you," which didn't sound right, but it was all that would come out. "Thank you, thank you."

One of my Michigan friends, Jason, steered me by the arm into the sanctuary. He'd morphed, in the couple of years since I'd last seen him, into a carpool dad. "Are you okay?" he said.

"No."

That morning when I'd put on my suit I'd found a mono-grammed paper napkin in my jacket pocket from a wedding that Hannah and I had gone to in Palm Springs that April *(Tim & Lizzie)*; as we walked I wadded it into a sweaty ball.

"Tell me if you need to turn around or anything," Jason said.

"I think I need to throw up."

"Really?"

"I don't know."

I'm not sure how I'd failed to understand that Hannah's casket was going to be on display. It was up at the front of the sanctuary, right in the center, on a stand with wheels, a shiny dark box with brass poles and a white cloth. My Valium evaporated. Jason evaporated. The Rampes had saved me a seat in the front row, but I couldn't take a step—the casket felt like a too-close bonfire.

Please don't let her actual body be in there. Please. Let this be a symbol, a Jewish version of communion wafers. Let her body be elsewhere, or nowhere, please. I told Jason that I needed to turn around, but he hesitated and then an usher appeared and before I could say anything I was being dragged the last hundred feet to the Rampes.

The rabbi stood staring down at his podium. "... Just this morning, Terri asked me how the Lord could let such a thing happen, and I had to tell her that I don't know. The ways of ..."

Almost every single person at a funeral believes that their being there is a kind of lie, that while everyone else is feeling the exact degree of grief recommended by the American Psychiatric Association, they alone are worrying about whether this will end in time for them to make their train.

I'd been at funerals like that. I'd never been at a funeral like this, which is to say: shaking, weeping, unable to follow more than ten seconds of what anyone said. I have the impression that I kept having to stand up, and that people were hugging me, but I can't really say.

"... When Hannah and I were just about to graduate ..."

"... She was always the cool one, the one us younger cousins wanted to be like ..."

I do remember the end, though. The pallbearers—three of

Hannah's uncles and a stone-faced family friend—rolled the casket down the aisle toward the lobby, slow as a dirge, and all of us who'd been sitting in the front row walked out behind them. *Hannah is in that box. Hannah is in that box.* An aunt of Hannah's that I barely knew was clutching my arm, sobbing. The Rampes—Bruce, Terri, and Megan—walked just in front of me, and they could barely get themselves down the aisle; they staggered along, holding each other up. The looks they gave the crowd—people in the aisles kept reaching out to touch them, to touch me—weren't accusatory, but cornered, as if we were wild animals caught in a trap.

This is our wedding, Hannah, I thought—and somehow that, imagining these rows of friends and cousins applauding instead of sobbing, cameras flashing instead of faces breaking, was the worst single moment I'd had since she disappeared. My legs went wobbly. The floor of my stomach dropped. Multiple hands appeared bearing water bottles.

At the cemetery, which was more than an hour away, in Long Island, there were bare trees and brown hills and so, so many graves. The hearse pulled up at the crest of a hill to a fake-grass carpet that led through the trees to Hannah's plot. It had gotten cold enough that everyone was wearing their winter coats over their suits and dresses. Megan had had a panic attack in the car and she sat fanning herself on a bench, being tended to by the same aunt who'd walked me out of the sanctuary.

"... Burial is a sacrament that allows the ..."

There were only ten or twenty chairs set up in front of the grave, so most people stood clustered on the sides, crying, crossing their arms. The Rampes and I sat in the front row. Bruce was sobbing, bouncing, barely making a sound. Terri was wailing. Megan pounded her fists against her legs. We looked, I remember thinking, like a line of prisoners facing the firing squad.

The hole was deep enough that I couldn't see the casket at

the bottom. The rabbi was still talking, but no one could hear him, his microphone was bad and the wind was making the tent flap, and it didn't matter.

Burial is so brutal. We are apes, we are animals, we grunt and grope and scratch our names in the dirt and then we get dumped in pits like luau pigs.

"… And now, in keeping with Jewish tradition, if anyone would like to …"

I was back in my mom's rental car, waiting for the heat to thaw out my hands, when I realized that everyone who'd been at the burial had left, everyone was back in their cars, except for Hannah, who was going to stay there in the ground, in these freezing woods, all through the night, and then the next night, and then the next thousand after that—that that's what this meant. My mom, pulling out, said, "Are you up for the reception? It's fine if you're not." I stretched out in the backseat and moaned.

[Edmund Wright's journal]

… William has now visited me on five of the past fourteen nights & whether I have lost hold of my senses or have ventured further into the world of spirits than Hodgkins ever dreamt, I cannot say. Sarah has made plain that I pursue this work in direct contravention of her wishes; I have made similarly plain that my temperament offers me no choice but to follow my researches where they lead me.

The first three encounters did in their bare outlines resemble the first: the solitude of the study, the sense & sound of another in the room, the liquid approach & the subsequent dissolution. On the night of his fourth return, however, I summoned the courage to stay fixed in my seat & the spirit, at the point when he had, on nights previous, disappeared, now touched my very skin & in so doing absorbed into me. The limits of language foreclose precision, but the feeling was as of being a dry rag placed into a cool liquid, & once it was done William, or this insubstantial distillation of him, seemed to inhabit the quarters where that which I call "I" customarily dwells. Never without laudanum have I stood so far from the banks of ordinary experience.

For a moment I sat awash with bliss, overcome by the sweetness of reunion—but before the feeling could ripen, my senses were immersed in a scene as horrible to me as it was familiar. Here was the road by our house, here was the gray October evening, here was the resting carriage, here stood Smuggler tall & noble. Notably I was not myself but William in this vision & so it was as my son, racing across the lawn & then mounting the wheel, that I lived the horror I shall not here record, terminating in a blackness whose depths I cannot approximate.

When I came to at my desk no more than a few minutes had passed; my papers were speckled in perspiration & my shirt was sopping. Such, I told myself, are the wages of progress. As the naturalist at sea clutches the railing & fixes his eyes on the horizon, so shall I endure . . .

Summer 2031—Connecticut—Age 50

You are standing in the shower bare bright red feet under scalding water you rub the soap against the washcloth start with your left arm stomach chest always the same the body moving without thought spinning like a car on an assembly line even this thought you've had how many hundreds of mornings how much of life is like this now the shampoo fingers through hair eyes scrunched your son calls from the living room Mom I'm leaving his voice is deeper now than his father's deeper somehow than it will eventually end up you call out okay and hope he doesn't hear your fear that he too will stand numb under who knows how many hundreds of showers you scrub the long scar on your stomach the pale splotch on your thigh you hear the door close downstairs you turn off the water and stand dripping for a second thinking this can't be what a person is for you must be tired you must have had too much to drink last night you reach without looking for the towel . . .

2

The strange thing—the thing the grief books all tell you but that you can't quite believe until you experience it—is that the first days are horrendous, and then the next bit is worse. Those days right after the funeral, during which I thought I'd felt as bad as it was humanly possible to feel, I'd been numbed, it turned out; what I'd been feeling was only half strength. And whatever those numbing chemicals had been—the same ones my body would have deployed if my leg had been torn off by a lion—I only had a few days' supply.

One of the main things I'd been numb to, it turned out, was my suspicion that Hannah had killed herself. I drifted around the city for a week or so after I checked out of the hotel—a few nights with an old music friend in Washington Heights, one night with a cousin of my dad's on East Sixty-seventh Street—and the question of Hannah's death came up in me like a rash. It was all I could think about; it was waiting to pounce on me at the end of every mental hallway. I'd wake up from a dream in which I'd found Hannah hanging from a beam in the Wright House, and then I'd spend the rest of the night—you can't fathom how long these nights were, sweating in strange beds—tormenting myself with even worse images: her bloated corpse, her face gasping for air, her hair floating like river weeds.

Of course I couldn't tell anyone about any of this—the thought of Hannah having killed herself felt literally unspeakable. My friends and parents had enough trouble knowing what to say to me as it was, and the Rampes—I went to see them most days, since I had nowhere else to go—seemed to be staggering on in their own grief-blind obliviousness. So I sweated, and I read nightmarish online message boards about suicide, and I carried on an endless court case entirely within the confines of my head: *She would have left a note, she wouldn't have left a note, what about the canoe, what about the Risperdal, she would never, you don't know . . .*

In the middle of this, the Rampes told me I could move in with them. This was a Wednesday in the first week in December. I'd spent the day at their apartment helping them go through condolence cards, and now I was ostensibly taking a nap in the guest room while they decided what to do about dinner.

Bruce came in and sat down next to me on the edge of the unmade bed. I hadn't been asleep, of course. The guest room happened to be where the laundry machines were, so the dryer was chugging and shushing a few feet away from us.

"You know you're welcome to stay here with us," Bruce said.

Instead of answering, I burst into tears—this was, fortunately, as unremarkable an act in their apartment as sneezing—and Bruce, not understanding that my tears meant *Dear God help me I think your daughter killed herself,* uneasily touched my shoulder before standing up.

Living at the Rampes' seemed, at first, to help somewhat with my suicide obsession. It wasn't that the thoughts about Hannah's death went away, but they lowered to a semi-tolerable volume. Dozens of times a day I told myself that if it were actually a rational thing to be thinking about, if this weren't just a cruel habit that my exhausted mind had fallen into, then the Rampes would have brought it up. *The grief-stricken mind is unusually vulnerable to delusions and misperceptions.* Where had I read that? Anyway, Bruce and Terri had known Hannah at least as well as I had. Their sense of her psyche was just as good as mine. If they weren't worried, then I shouldn't be worried. All the things I'd resisted believing with all my strength when she was alive, I now flung myself into like a baptismal bath.

I wasn't the only extra person in the apartment; Megan, Hannah's sister, had decided to stick around too. This was less of a problem than it might have been. Megan had always been the trouble daughter: rehab, credit card debt, the disastrous marriage. For the first couple of years that I'd known the Rampes, Megan could be counted on to contribute at least one drunken, tearful fight to every family gathering. Now she seemed to be in a good phase—the purple half-moons were gone from under her eyes; her hair was a more or less normal color. In her reconfigured family, she seemed to have taken on the role of caretaker. She'd venture out to CVS or Fairway when our supplies of pills or food ran low. She would force smoothies on us (she'd once worked at a health food store in Providence, and had an abiding faith in kefir and matcha powder); she'd turn on lamps whenever we found ourselves just sitting in the dark. "You look bad, Dad," she said. "I'm getting you some tea." I'm reluctant to say anything positive about the feeling in the apartment, because the baseline was so awful, but there was—compared, anyway, with suffering alone on my college friend's futon—something almost cozy about it, recuperative, a sense of huddling around a fire on an inhospitable planet.

And conversation in the apartment, just like conversation around a campfire, came mostly in gusts between silences, addressed partly to whoever happened to be sitting nearby and partly to the air. One night the four of us were sitting in the living room—we'd finished a dinner Megan had made of Moroccan chicken, and we were working our way through a second bottle of wine—when Terri told a story.

"You know what, years ago, this must have been five years ago—which probably means it was ten years ago—a girl in

Hannah's class at Oberlin died, I think her name was Nicole. Beautiful girl, very waifish, almost see-through skin. She was with a boy who'd had too much to drink and he'd driven off the road and of course he'd walked away fine. And she'd been killed instantly. Or maybe she died the next day, I don't remember. You probably know, Megan. But in any event this happened, and she died, and of course it was an enormous deal for the entire school, Oberlin is very small, there were assemblies and they brought in counselors and the head of the school wrote us all emails about how our kids were coping and what we could do to help. This was the first death, the first death of a peer, that lots of them had ever dealt with. I think they decided to rename a room in the library after her, the Nicole-something reading room.

"And I remember having the thought, I remember it very vividly, I was right here in this room: *So, that's the one.* Because every class, every group of kids when they're growing up, has to have their little tragedy. In my class it was Lewis McKay. For Megan it was John Wolff. These things are shocking, but they're also predictable, in a funny way: you expect to be shocked at some point. And if it was Nicole, for Hannah's group, then it wasn't going to be Hannah. Like a lightning rod. I don't think I quite put it to myself like that, but that is how you think, as a parent."

She stopped for long enough that I thought she was finished, but she wasn't, quite.

"I remember feeling guilty about it at the time," she said, looking over at Bruce. "Well." She took a big gulp of wine. "Not guilty enough."

. . .

Hannah's old bedroom had, at some point since her death, become a memorial. The bed in which Hannah and I had slept on the rare occasions when we'd stayed with the Rampes'—in which we'd had quiet sex and wrestled over the fan remote and stayed up watching *Inspector Morse* on her laptop—was now covered in the stuffed animals Hannah had collected when she was eight. There were framed photos of her on every surface, from every phase of her life—grinning in a strappy black dress at a work event; bravely bearing braces against a pastel-blue background; in a bikini on a beach with Megan. Terri would spend hours in there each day weeping over old yearbooks, sorting through T-shirts. Bruce would sometimes wander in and spin slowly in a baffled circle, like a little boy lost in Tokyo.

At first I couldn't bear going in there—among the many things that had become poison to me, photos of her were possibly the worst—but after I'd been at the Rampes' for a week or so I gave in. There turned out to be a not-unpleasant enfoldingness about it. I still didn't look directly at the pictures of her, but I wandered around picking things up, quietly marveling. This was where she'd slept every night for the first eighteen years of her life. This was where she'd talked on the phone to boyfriends with forehead acne. Every single thing—the blue plaid blanket with "FRIENDS SEMINARY" sewed into it; the black plastic alarm clock with the wires poking out; the tower of empty CD cases—had had some significance to her, had seemed worth saving. It was, I eventually realized, like being in a historic house museum.

And then I did force myself to look at the pictures: not the recent ones, not the ones in which she looked like the Hannah I'd been engaged to, but the old ones—six-year-old Hannah standing at a sink in her grandparents' house in Connecticut, helping to wash a bowl full of lettuce; eleven-year-old Hannah at camp, working on a stick-and-feather dreamcatcher.

This is what I was doing—sitting on Hannah's bed, sipping a glass of Bruce's Scotch, flipping through an album of photos of fifth-grade Hannah in an apple orchard—when Megan walked in and closed the door. It was eleven thirty on a Tuesday night.

"Can I talk to you for a second?"

"Okay."

She squinted at me. We hadn't been alone in a room together the whole time we'd been in the apartment.

"When are you going to stop bullshitting everyone?"

For a second my brain was startled into flashbulb blankness. So this was the old, bad Megan. It was as if she'd been acting in a play and we were now backstage. Her eyes and her voice made me think she'd been drinking. I asked her what she was talking about.

"I talked to Hannah's doctor this afternoon."

I just looked at her.

"Dr. Blythe. He said he talked to her a few times before she died. He said he'd been worried about her."

"Okay," I said. My heart had started to kick.

"And *I* talked to Hannah a couple of days before she died. You didn't know that, did you? Something was off. I could tell. What was wrong with her? Tell me."

"What did you talk to her about?"

She waved her hand, like someone clearing away a cobweb.

"We talked about bullshit—my job, Thanksgiving, the wedding. She was holding back, though. She was gonna tell me something."

"What do you think she was going to tell you?"

Megan hesitated, looked away, seemed to forget I was in the room. Then she asked, in a drunken approximation of a whisper, "Did she kill herself?"

It was the first time I'd heard anyone say the words out loud. "You don't know what you're talking about," I said.

"I'm right, though, aren't I? Dr. Blythe wouldn't say it, but I will. I thought about it as soon as I heard she was dead, but then I told myself she couldn't have, Nick would have to know. But then I thought, maybe you *do* know. So just tell me, okay? I won't say anything to my parents. Did she kill herself?"

"You need to go to sleep."

"So you haven't thought about it for one second?"

I lied as automatically as a child. "Correct," I said.

Megan fixed her eyes on me. "If my parents weren't already a fucking wreck, I would press you on this, okay? I know you're not telling us something."

And she left me alone with my empty glass and my photo album.

Back in the guest room I didn't sleep that night: the rash of unwelcome thoughts had become my entire skin. I tried, uselessly, to remind myself of all the ways in which Megan was insane—the YouTube documentary she'd made me and Hannah watch about how the Denver airport was actually an internment camp; her belief that half of the world's problems were due to a vitamin B_{12} deficiency. But it didn't matter. Every thought I'd ever had about Hannah's death returned to me now in a meticulous *how-could-you-ever-have-doubted-it?* edit. Her breakdown when we were putting up Halloween decorations. The full medicine bottle. The farewell sex. I shook so hard, lying there with the sheets wrapped around me, that I could hear the bed frame rattling against the wall.

But morning always comes, no matter what sort of night you've had; this is an underappreciated fact. I splashed my face at the sink in the little guest room bathroom and brushed my tongue and told myself: *Bruce and Terri know that Hannah's death was an accident, and that's all that matters. Get through today, give nothing to Megan, and let everyone, including yourself, get on with their heartbroken lives.* I walked out into the rest of the apartment with my throbbing head held high.

I've tried to understand now why it was so unthinkable to me to just tell the Rampes the truth—why couldn't I just have said that I had a terrible suspicion that Hannah might have killed herself, and that this was at least as excruciating a possibility to me as it was to them? Why did I have to compound my troubles by acting like a criminal? The only answer I can come up with— the only answer that isn't implausibly self-flattering—is that I *felt* like a criminal: the fiancé is never entirely innocent. If Hannah had killed herself, then I had destroyed the Rampes' lives— not to mention my life—with an obliviousness that deserved jail or worse.

Anyway, as soon as I walked into the kitchen, I could feel that my plans for the day were beside the point. It was close to nine thirty. Bruce was on the phone, standing at the island with a pen and note pad; Terri was at her desk in the corner, gazing at the computer. Neither of them looked up when I walked in, or gave any indication that they were aware of me at all, so I must have seen something in their faces, felt a kind of tightness in the air.

I didn't notice that Megan had walked into the kitchen until she spoke from right behind me. "I changed my mind. I had them call Dr. Blythe this morning," she said. "You can tell them why you think we're full of bullshit."

Now Bruce and Terri were facing me—Bruce had set down

the phone and he was polishing his glasses, which was for some reason as terrifying as if he'd been sharpening a hunting knife.

"Is there something you haven't told us?" Terri asked. She sounded desperate.

"No," I said.

Bruce looked up. "Dr. Blythe wouldn't tell us much, but he said this morning that Hannah hadn't refilled her medicine since September. Did you know that?"

"She was taking something else," I said.

"Not according to Dr. Blythe, she wasn't." His voice was deadly calm.

"She was going to see him when we came for Thanksgiving," I said.

"He didn't know that. He said they'd only had a few phone appointments."

Bruce was moving forward as he spoke, so when he asked me if I was absolutely *sure* there was nothing I wanted to tell him, he was standing close enough that I could smell the coffee on his breath. I sputtered out, "I thought she was okay."

The rest of the conversation—Bruce advancing, me retreating, Terri and Megan orbiting like referees—couldn't have lasted for more than ten minutes, but it felt eternal, outside of time.

Bruce: "The moment you knew she wasn't taking her medicine, that's when you should have called us. The *second* you understood that something might have been the matter."

Me: "I didn't think something was the matter. I didn't know."

Terri: "But if you even had to think about it, why didn't you *say* something to us? Why didn't you tell us you were worried?"

Me: "I wasn't worried. I thought she was okay."

Bruce: "What did I say to you before you moved away? What did I tell you, standing right here in the kitchen?"

Terri: "Just tell us if she was all right or if there was something going on with her. Just tell us that."

Me: "She was having a hard time. It was a stressful couple of months."

Terri (now sobbing): "Then why didn't you tell us?! Our baby may have killed herself! *Killed* herself! Can you imagine the pain she must have been in? And you were right there and you could have called someone, you could have called us, but you did nothing, you just came here and you—"

Megan: "You fucking sat there while everybody said *What a terrible accident*, and you just sat there and you—"

Bruce: "You let us down. We trusted you with the thing we value most in the world and you destroyed it. You destroyed us."

Terri: "How did this happen? Please, please, tell me, how did this happen?"

By this point the three of them had literally backed me into a corner, in front of the coat closet, and I was all but shielding my face.

"I don't know how it happened," I said. "I don't know." And this, I realized, scrabbling backward along the wall, nearly knocking over a side table, was—unlike almost everything else I'd said recently—entirely true.

No one had to tell me that I wasn't welcome at the Rampes' anymore. That morning I went back into the guest room, stuffed my things into my duffel bag, and, with no goodbye and no sense of where I might be headed, walked out into the middle of a cold gray rain on Broadway.

You can't understand, until you've lost someone, what a horrendous assault New York City is capable of committing on a person's senses. Sleeplessness must have been part of it. Also I hadn't really been out on the street, for any extended period, since Hannah's death—and before that, I hadn't been back to the city since August. It was freezing now, wet and grim and Thanksgiving-decorated. But that didn't mean the streets weren't teeming with activity. Tourists lined up outside the CBS building for a glimpse of someone in a camel's-hair coat and heavy makeup. A small Indian woman next to a Starbucks truck was offering samples of a chocolate drink in elf-sized paper cups. A hellish proliferation of women Hannah's age, all obnoxiously alive, walked past me in every direction, hoods tightened around their faces, yoga mats strapped to their backs. Every single advertising poster and scaffolding bar and store window seemed to say: No one ever dies and nothing ever ends and no one has ever suffered anything worse than a cracked iPhone screen.

I walked into Central Park near Columbus Circle, and, suddenly woozy, settled in with my bag on a clammy wooden bench near the pond. On the bench a few to my left there was a heap of black garbage bags that might or might not have concealed a person. My right sock was soaked from a puddle. So this, I thought, is how homelessness begins, not with a momentous decision but with a gradual surrendering; a rest becomes a nap becomes a night. It only occurred to me as I was arranging my duffel bag into a pillow that there was in fact one place in the city I could go—one place, that is, where I could go without risking hypothermia or institutionalization. Hannah's and my old car was still sitting in the Rampes' garage.

I gathered my things and walked quickly back out of the park. It's amazing how eager you can be for the comforts of a fifteen-year-old Volvo. The car key, a cracked black rubber square, was, I realized, the only key on my keychain that worked for any door I still had even the remotest interest in entering. Why hadn't it occurred to me weeks ago? I'd never need to call on the Rampes or some half-forgotten friend again; I would begin my life as a grief-powered nomad.

The garage attendant blinked at me indifferently from his stool. I found the car between a stone pillar and a white Lexus SUV. The doors were still splashed with dried mud that must have come from upstate, maybe the hike off the Taconic we'd taken in September. The car was cold enough, inside, that I could, sitting in the driver's seat, see my breath in front of my face. Hannah's tissues and lemon cough drops and sunglasses were still piled in the broken center console. A flyer from the Wright House's Spooky Halloween Festival was still tucked into the passenger's-side door. For the hundredth time since she'd died I was struck by the sloppiness of death, by the world's refusal to let you forget absolutely anything.

I pulled out of the garage—that the car started at all was a minor miracle—and for what must have been an hour I drove slowly around Manhattan with the balky heat turned up full blast. A sleepy-voiced woman on NPR was talking about the craft of memoir. Be sure to include lots of sensory details—that was the important thing, apparently. Also, don't forget to give your family fair warning. I switched to a half-clear bluegrass station. Periodically, as I drove, I felt water running from the corners of my eyes, but I didn't know if these were tears of feeling or tears of body-system malfunction. Driving in New York City is only unbearable, I realized, because you're usually trying to get somewhere. I drove down the Henry Hudson, wove for a while through Midtown, following the lights, then came back up along Sixth Avenue. I honked at a biker, experimentally, zoomed around a waiting cab. I was on a long Upper West Side block, passing an empty stretch of sidewalk, when it occurred to me—I felt an instant and horrifying sort of relief—that there was nothing keeping me from plowing directly into the stone side of one of these buildings. Would that be enough to kill me? Forty or fifty miles per hour, head on into a wall? My parents, my friends, the Rampes, a stranger watching NY1—would any of them really be surprised? A thirty-year-old man, whose fiancée recently drowned in a small town near Rhinebeck, was killed in a one-car accident on Tuesday afternoon. The lemon squares from Hannah's reception would get to serve double duty.

But my hands didn't turn the wheel—instead, I drove steadily on and turned left on Central Park West—and this was, I realized, not because of any instinct toward self-preservation. It was because if I crashed, I would never find out what Hannah had told Dr. Blythe. So this—the moment of not leaping my car onto the sidewalk, not having my rib cage crushed against the steering wheel—was when I first formulated to myself the choice that would become my mantra: I could either die or I could find out why Hannah had died. Curiosity is responsible for as many saved lives as penicillin.

I don't know if I'd been unconsciously driving toward Dr.

Blythe's office the whole time, or if it was more that the car was now obeying its own gravitational pull. In any case I was now passing Seventy-third Street. I knew, from things Hannah had said, that his office was somewhere in the West Eighties, and luckily, psychiatrists' addresses turn out to be no harder to find online than anyone else's. Dr. Albert Edward Blythe was at 9 West Eighty-fifth Street, Suite 5A, less than half a mile from the Rampes' apartment, less than three blocks from where I was. I had only the foggiest notion of what I intended to say to him— *Please tell me everything; please tell me only the things that suggest she died accidentally.* But I turned left on Eighty-fifth and there it was, a redbrick building with a green awning and, despite the season, air conditioners protruding from every other window. I parked with the back half of the Volvo hanging in front of a driveway and, doing a convincing impression of a man in need of psychiatric services, walked hurriedly past the doorman.

For as long as I'd known about Dr. Blythe, I had always— though of course I'd never mentioned this to Hannah—felt a mostly senseless dislike for him. I'd been eager for her to talk to him when she'd had her pre-Halloween meltdown, of course, but that had only been desperation. Therapists of significant others are always nodes of weird feeling, I think. They charge too much. They know too much. Even former therapists are like exes who've never quite been broken up with.

The building was a shabbier cousin of the Rampes'—brass mailboxes, tile floors, stacks of Amazon packages against a wall. As soon as I stepped out of the elevator on the fifth floor, I could hear the collective roar of a dozen white noise machines. Every floor in the building must have been like this; I was inside a beehive of mental anguish. I turned the knob on the door labeled 5A.

Dr. Blythe's waiting room was small and carpeted and windowless, Santa Fe anonymous. There were three or four black chairs, an abstract print of what looked like a totem pole, a glass table heaped with *National Geographics* and *New Yorkers*. One man sat waiting for his appointment—a weary-looking finance type who kept crossing and uncrossing his legs, sighing theatrically. I realized two things as I sat down: that multiple doctors shared this suite, and that I was, despite not having eaten since the night before, in more-than-theoretical danger of throwing up. I took a few deep breaths and closed my eyes. My first order of business was just to learn which of these doors was Dr. Blythe's. Whatever came next—introducing myself as Hannah's fiancé, pretending to be a detective from Hibernia, running out the door—I could worry about afterward. It was just before two o'clock.

One of the doctors in the suite, the first one I saw, was a bronze-haired sixty-ish woman wrapped in earth-toned scarves. She opened her door to let out a nervous-looking man with a backpack. The next doctor I saw was an athletic-looking gray-haired woman all in black; she came out to claim the finance guy. I noticed, after I'd watched some number of appointment transitions, that the doctors periodically went from their offices into a little room behind me. It wasn't a bathroom, I decided; no flushing sound came from inside. I couldn't see into it—the doctors all opened and closed the door as if there were a panther inside—but I thought that it had to be a shared kitchen. I pictured mugs in a cabinet next to old boxes of tea; a microwave splattered with dried dribbles of lunch. The scarf doctor came out of her office, smiled professionally, and stepped in there. Then a bald male doctor, one I hadn't seen yet, with his foot in a hi-tech black surgical boot. But still no Dr. Blythe.

By two forty-five I'd started to think that I might have been on the wrong floor, or that the picture I'd found on Google Images had been of a different Albert Blythe, and so maybe the bald man was Hannah's doctor after all. But then a fancily dressed woman walked out of the door right in front of me, the only door that hadn't already opened—I knew the woman wasn't the doctor, because she was dabbing at her eyes—and there, standing right behind her, tightly smiling in farewell, was Dr. Blythe.

It's always weird, seeing someone in person after having only seen them in a photograph. He wore a striped gray suit, and he looked a few years older than he had in the picture, baggier in the face and neck. My heart speed and vomit potential increased on parallel tracks. Dr. Blythe glanced toward me with an expression that said, *You aren't waiting for me, I hope?* I shook my head minimally. He reminded me of late-career Jimmy Stewart, a kindly small-town judge. He had thin lips and combed silver hair and round glasses. Hannah's most trusted repository for distress. He stepped past me into the mystery room and I, with my ears booming, fixed my eyes on the magazine in my lap.

Some part of me, I realized, had expected instant recognition—not that he'd know my particular identity, but that he'd know I was there on business related to Hannah's death; that he'd have spent the past couple of weeks consumed by the question of what had happened to her, ever ready to be interrogated. This had been craziness on my part, I realized now. He was a professional. And part of what his profession entailed was occasional disasters befalling his patients; crisis was the water in which he swam. The calls he'd gotten from Megan and Bruce probably hadn't even been the strangest interactions of his week. There was no way he'd be shamed or shocked into telling me details that he hadn't told them. He hadn't stepped out of his office and seen Hannah Rampe's grief-sick fiancé; he'd seen a damp, unshaven stranger who looked and smelled like he'd spent the past twenty-four hours on a Greyhound bus. He was probably in that little room calling the doorman to see why I'd been let up.

So I did finally have a plan, I realized. If I was going to get anything of value from Dr. Blythe, I was going to have to steal it.

There were, at that point, two other people with me in the waiting room—a skeletal teenage girl reading a *Game of Thrones* paperback so thick it was almost cubic, and a fortysomething woman with curly hair and glasses who I took to be the skeleton's mother. Probably the mom had caught the daughter throwing up. Or maybe she'd caught her with an older guy. Anyway they seemed too preoccupied by their own suffering to interfere with mine. It was now almost three o'clock.

For most of the time that I'd been sitting there I'd been reading, or pretending to read, an article in a year-old issue of *National Geographic* about Pygmies in Brazil. What I was going to do now, I decided, was close the magazine, stand up, and, while Dr. Blythe was busy enjoying his cup of tea, calmly try the door to his office. If it was locked—or if another doctor walked out and saw me breaking protocol—I'd say something sheepish about this being my first appointment. All the other doors in the suite were still closed. I could hear what I was fairly sure was Dr. Blythe's soft voice through the door behind me, a friendly murmur. I'll do it in three seconds, I told myself. Two seconds. Pygmies subsist almost entirely on bushmeat. Now.

The door to Dr. Blythe's office wasn't locked, and neither was the inner one—two doors, just a couple of feet apart from each other. I twisted the bolts on both of them behind me. I was too single-minded, too adrenalized, once I was inside the office, to reflect on the fact that this was where Hannah had spent who knows how many hours pouring out her secrets. I was making a steady, urgent, just-going-about-my-business hum. The room smelled strongly of sandalwood. I pulled open a drawer in the large mahogany desk—pens and paper clips. A half-dead spider plant stood in the far corner; a box of tissues sat on a glossy black side table. I sifted through a pile of journals and envelopes on the edge of the desk; nothing, nothing. But there—between the desk and the wall, at knee height, was a gray metal filing cabinet.

Yes. The drawers were locked, but after a couple of minutes of prying and wiggling with one of the paper clips—shades of high school gym lockers—I managed to spring the top one open, and then the bottom.

Whatever I may have thought about Dr. Blythe, I couldn't accuse him of sloppiness. In each drawer there were dozens of manila files, all hanging neatly with his patients' names and treatment dates handwritten on white labels in his careful script. Anders, Deborah, 1/15/98–4/21/03. Clustig, Anthony, 7/20/97–9/6/98. Inside the files were bills and insurance forms and handwritten notes on yellow lined paper.

Hannah's file was in the bottom drawer, toward the back. Rampe, Hannah, 6/17/05–. He hadn't gotten around to filling out the end date.

I'd just lifted her file out of the drawer when I heard someone trying the outer door. Either that or I'd bumped into something. Then the knocking started—tentative at first, almost embarrassed, but harder with each passing second. *"Who's in there?"*

I didn't answer.

"Let me in there this second!"

I still didn't answer. My heart was ticking, quickly but quietly. I glanced out the window, saw that there was no fire escape, realized that it would have been insane to use it anyway. My nausea had disappeared. I knew what I needed to do; I just needed to sort out the choreography. I tucked Hannah's file into the front of my pants, pulled my shirt over it, took a deep breath, and opened the inner door. Now I could hear Dr. Blythe much more clearly, just a foot away from me, right on the other side of the outer door. *"If you don't let me in right now I'm going to—"*

But I never learned what he was going to do. Instead, in one motion, I unlocked the door and burst through it like a rushing linebacker. Dr. Blythe fell backward into the table with the magazines, then slid down onto the floor. His glasses were off. His hair was mussed.

For a second he crawled around on all fours, like a boxer struggling to find the ropes, and I just stood there frozen. The curly-haired woman was on her feet, trying to help Dr. Blythe up, while the daughter sat staring at me wide-eyed. "For God's sake, Caitlyn, call 911," the mother said.

But by then I'd been reanimated. I was out the door, down the stairs, and back in my car, before she could even have explained the emergency.

[Edmund Wright's journal]

… Though Sarah insists, with increasing fervor & despair, that I grow gaunt & sallow, never have I made such leaps in comprehension as I have in these recent weeks; damn the body & its continued pleas for tending.

The first break came quite by accident; on the evening of William's eighth visit, I happened not to set down the pencil I had in hand as he approached. Thus did I wake, after the customary vision, to find that while living out William's death in mind, I had also set down a page-long account of it on paper. Thus began my training as a scribe for the spirits.

And this was not even my most momentous turn—for last Monday evening I sensed, sitting in my study, that behind me milled not just William but a whole company of beings, & sure enough, when the time came for my inhabitation, it was not William's spirit I recognized & it was not William's death into which I was immersed. Our home, I realized, may be host to a veritable multitude. Crouching in near every household object, I now believe, hide spirits like snakes in the crevices of a stone wall, each one awaiting a suitable vessel into which they might, for the time being, slip & through which they might find expression. Having been carved into just such a ready vessel by William's visitations, I now find myself deluged, nightly, by more spirits than I can here record. There was, four nights past, the sorry fellow who met his end in the thresher at the mill; the following night came the woodland creature (for the spiritual world seems to be no more exclusively the domain of man than does the biological world) who came to grief in the jaws of a coyote. Thus do I, proud researcher & man of letters, find my calling as acting secretary for an invisible & insubstantial assembly.

I report without boastfulness that during these fruitful weeks my capacity for sustaining periods of inhabitation has grown prodigiously. The visitations now last an hour or more; the accounts that I wake to find filling my notebook contain evermore detail, evermore clarity.

Thus must I guard against complacency & stay ever mindful of the staggering volume of questions still to be explored, viz., Are spirits unhappy, reliving their deaths day & night? Do they long to escape from their peculiar state? Do they desire more from living beings than temporary fleshly homes, & if so, what is their desiderata?

. . .

[*Poughkeepsie Journal,* January 5, 1958]

DUTCHESS COUNTY WOMAN
GOES MISSING FROM HIBERNIA HOME
Friends and Family Pray for Her Safety

Hibernia, January 5, 1958—Dutchess County Sheriff Richard Thornhill asked the public for assistance on Sunday in locating Hibernia resident Janet Kemp, missing since New Year's Day. Mrs. Kemp, a 40-year-old homemaker and mother of three, was reported missing by her husband, George Kemp, on the evening of the 1st and has not been seen since.

"We continue to hope that Mrs. Kemp will be reunited with her family," said Sheriff Thornhill. "In the meantime we're asking anyone with any information to please step forward." Sheriff Thornhill acknowledged that the weekend's snow has made his department's search all the more challenging.

Mrs. Kemp is known as a valued community member and the proud mother of three children, ages 10, 6, and 5, all enrolled at Cold Spring Elementary. Her husband is one of Hibernia's two family physicians, with a specialty in obstetric care. The Kemp family has been described by neighbors as unusually kind and generous. Their support was instrumental in the construction of the new Town Hall on Cold Spring Road.

On the day of Mrs. Kemp's disappearance, the Kemps visited a neighbor, and they were seen returning home no later than 4 o'clock in the afternoon. The neighbor whom they visited, Alfred Creswell, described the Kemps' behavior that day as being entirely ordinary. "Only thing I can remember is that George kept wanting to know whether I thought the snow would hold off," said Creswell.

The Kemp home, located at 23 Culver Road, is one of Hibernia's oldest, dating back to the years before the American Revolution. The house and its environs were thoroughly searched by Sheriff Thornhill and his officers immediately after Mrs. Kemp's disappearance. On Thursday afternoon a neighbor drew the police's attention to a shovel left standing in the woods beside the house, but upon questioning Mr. Kemp explained that the shovel belonged to his eldest daughter, who had used it to bury a doll. No further evidence was discovered.

Mrs. Kemp's disappearance and the subsequent investigation have created a palpable sense of unease in the ordinarily tranquil Hibernia. "We are heartsick when we think what could have happened to Jan," said one neighbor, who asked not to be identified. "Especially with this cold. We want so much to believe this will all end happily."

Among those who have not given up hope is Mr. Kemp, who stood alongside Sheriff Thornhill on Tuesday and seconded the sheriff's call to the public for information. "We miss Jan terribly," Mr. Kemp said, "and we will not rest until she is back home with her family." Asked by a reporter if he felt unsafe, living in the house from which his wife disappeared, Mr. Kemp answered succinctly. "I do not," he said.

3

There's a short list of things that, in the interest of harmony and sanity, all couples should be forbidden to do: walking in on the other in the bathroom; thinking in any real detail about the other's prior sex life; sharing more than the shallowest of one's insights regarding the other's parents. To this list of terrible ideas I'd now like to add: reading the other's psychiatric notes.

Before I could make that particular mistake, though, I needed to get away. I drove from Dr. Blythe's office—an orange-enveloped parking ticket flapping on my windshield—up Columbus, past the red stone church that Hannah and I had once had a fight in front of, past the scaffolding-covered building that Terri called the scourge of the Upper West Side. There's a feeling, a hot, pulsating busyness, that goes with having done something you know is going to get you in trouble—it goes back to elementary school, the terror of a teacher's footsteps; or it may go back even further than that, savannah sins. Anyway, I had it, I was dizzy with it. Every part of me that wasn't directly involved in the act of driving was shaking. I was doing the vehicular equivalent of the fake-casual walking people do when they're trying not to look suspicious. I stopped at every light that seemed even to be thinking about turning yellow; I used my turn signal with greater precision and patience than I had since my driver's test. Hannah's file lay in the empty passenger's seat next to me, and I reached over and covered it with my jacket as if it were a bundle of dynamite.

My initial plan was to circle around for a bit and then to drive to the Rampes', where I'd put the car back in the garage and present Bruce and Terri with Dr. Blythe's notes, thereby demonstrating that I was in exactly the same position that they were—hiding nothing, desperate to know the truth. But of course the police—if the curly-haired woman or her daughter had really called them—would already have found out whose file it was that had been taken. So the Rampes' apartment, of all the places in the city, was probably the one where it made the least sense for me to go right then.

Yes, I practice-murmured, turning left on Ninety-sixth, *I am the late Hannah Rampe's fiancé, but no, I have no idea who stole her file or decked her psychiatrist. Maybe it was a crazy person who read about her in the news. Maybe it was her sister.* What were the chances that this would put off even the dimmest of cops? I drove past Amsterdam, did my best to ignore a dog walker in a purple poncho who I was fairly sure was pointing at my license plate. Maybe it would be better if I just fessed up and claimed to have been temporarily insane? Was it really so untrue? A road worker in a neon vest flapped his flag and bared his teeth at me. I was now merging onto the Henry Hudson, and as I eased up to the toll booths, I had the thought—this actually formed itself in the sweaty elevator that was my mind—that I needed to remember to ask Hannah if she'd refilled the EZ Pass.

I ended up pulling over to read the notes, finally, at a sandwich place in a strip mall somewhere off the Saw Mill, deep in a suburban-feeling section of the Bronx. I'd been driving by then for thirty or maybe forty minutes. Sustained panic is, above all, exhausting—my hands were numb from gripping the wheel; my legs were cramped and tense; my head seemed to have been stuffed with fiberglass batting. There was a parking lot behind the strip mall, a grim little row of rear entrances. *The suspect was apprehended in an empty deli between a tanning salon and a physical therapist's office ...*

"Welcome to Gino's! What can I get you?" The girl behind the counter was in her early twenties, pink streaks in her hair, valiantly cheerful. A copy of *The Five Love Languages* was splayed next to the register.

"Just some coffee."

"Anything else for you today?"

"Just the coffee."

Opening Hannah's folder ended up requiring a greater act of will than breaking into Dr. Blythe's office had. Until that moment, gulping bitter coffee with the manila folder on the table in front of me, I'd managed to keep my thoughts away from the question of what I might actually find in the notes. My hands were shaking. My chest was heaving. The girl behind the counter looked over, seeming to sense that I was in some sort of extremis, and I gave her a look meant to convey that everything was fine, or in any case that mine was a not-fine-ness that I could deal with myself. I think I was half-hoping that the folder would turn out to have nothing in it but Xeroxed bills and prescription records.

No such luck. The first page of notes—there were maybe thirty or forty pages total—was from Hannah's first appointment with Dr. Blythe, her consultation, in June of 2005, in the middle of her postcollege breakdown. Dr. Blythe's handwriting was small and precise and forward leaning, like some futuristic font.

6/17

Healthy, charismatic, attractive. No trouble meeting eyes. Describes situation ("why I'm here, I guess") w/ slight embarrassment, distance.

Says sleep probs (6–9 months), trouble both falling asleep & staying asleep. Loss of app. Loss of interest in friends, ord activities (works @ law office, used to enjoy, now dreads). Sudden eps of extreme fear, heart racing, sensation of imm disaster, esp at night. Very bad past 1–2 mos (6–7 disturbed nights/week). Lived w/ roommate, fem friend from coll (Oberlin), now back w/ parents (Upper WS), w/ whom she's close

To have someone you love die is to be under the recurrent impression that until right that moment, you haven't actually appreciated the enormity of what's happened; that the real suffering can only begin *now*. This, sitting quaking at a wobbly metal table somewhere in the Bronx, was one of those moments. The sky was now dark enough that I could see myself in the restaurant's windows. My knees were literally knocking. And here in my hands was Hannah, twenty-three-year-old Hannah, alive and scared and seeking help.

6/24

Dad, Bruce, v controlling, formid, mid-50's (surgeon)—H has great respect, slight fear; Mom, Terri, once in PR, 58, nervous (hist of dysthy, poss meds (Welb?), poss postp—> H's birth)—H feels protective, symp. Both p's place major value/pressure on education, accomp, etc.

Sis, Megan, 2 yrs older, bl sheep, hard teen years—> adulthood, subs abuse (alc, mar), H feels guilt/concern/excess respons, "the good daughter"

The notes went on like this, page after page, sessions from all that summer and fall, like a biography written in shorthand and then thrown in a blender.

7/26

H was 8 or 9—walked in, Terri weeping (poss post g-mother's death; associated w/ that news)—> H concludes: undependable, parent w/ out emotional resources to take prop care. Persistent belief. Burden.

9/2

Setback, maj anx attack on train Weds PM: was reading article re heart transplant, decided was herself having med incident w/ heart or brain (had thought might be psychosom, fear re "what if it's not?"). Once off train, humiliation, self-blame, "something wrong w/ me," "nothing helps," v disturbed sleep. Poss phobia developing re confinement, esp underground. Add 5mg Lexapro?

10/14

H tells (w/ strong trep, embarrassment) recurrent childhood night-fear: something crouching in laundry hamper, could hear it breathing/scratching, H knew thing was horr beyond describing, sent to punish her for unnamed sins (puritanism), couldn't call to p's or sis—> shame of having to expl reason for thing's presence (also: sense they wouldn't be able to help?)

The first batch of notes ended in November of that year. She'd been seeing Dr. Blythe once a week or so to that point, and now, apparently, she took a break; she seemed to have been feeling better—on a regimen of pills, living on her own. So this was the Hannah that I'd met: fresh from a rough patch, tentatively on her feet—and, to outward appearances, as content and self-assured as a woman in a shampoo ad.

The next set of notes—the ones that referred to anything more substantive than a prescription refill or a dosage tweak—came from a year and a half later, in the spring of '07. Hannah had gone back in to see Dr. Blythe because she'd had another panic attack, this one at work.

5/5

H in meeting, felt prickle in palms, sense of being v far from own body, then sudd sense of emergency, heart "a balloon about to burst." Coworkers staring—> made worse. Temp inability to speak. Ep lasted approx 3 mins.

The thing was, though: Hannah and I had been dating in the spring of '07. Not living together, yet, but spending almost every night together, as involved in each other's lives, as aware of each other's doings, as if we'd been married. This had been our period of elaborate-meal cooking and street-corner kissing. I *remembered* when she'd had this panic attack, and it hadn't been at all the way the notes described it—or at least the notes had the emphasis all wrong. She'd been dehydrated that day, hadn't eaten breakfast, and, sitting in an endless hot exhibit meeting, had started feeling like she might faint. She'd called me as soon as she'd gotten back to her desk. I remembered us standing in the narrow kitchen of her apartment that night, Hannah with a jumbo bottle of yellow Powerade, and both of us joking about getting her a Life Alert necklace. And yet:

5/9

Describes terror/shame during night following attack—> re "what if something is badly wrong"—psych if not phys ("maybe the medicine isn't working"). Had old nightmare of inner orgs being made of something soft, "like paste," sense of falling apart. Incr fear of trying to sleep.

What I felt, reading this and the pages after, was a more distressing version of the thing you feel when you catch a glimpse of yourself on a store's surveillance TV. Does my hair really do that in the back? Could that slump-shouldered stranger really be me? The Hannah in Dr. Blythe's notes was so much sadder and more fearful and less stable than the person I'd been dating. My Hannah would have taken this Hannah out for lunch and given her hours of wise advice. Either she'd given Dr. Blythe a serious misimpression or I'd spent the beginning of our relationship— maybe all of our relationship—in an oblivious fog.

This, I thought, finishing my coffee, reading yet another page about her panic and night terrors, was as painful as things would get—and then I turned to the pages from when we were living at Wright. I could have, and probably should have, started with these pages, I knew, but something had stopped me; some suffering can only be approached on tiptoe.

The first call Hannah made to Dr. Blythe when we were living at Wright really had been the night of the meltdown out by the graves—in this, at least, my version of things did line up with the notes. But Hannah hadn't just called Dr. Blythe to make an appointment for when we were back in the city, or to talk to him about her medicine; she'd wanted to tell him something. She'd called him again the next morning. They'd had multiple full-length sessions over the phone during the next couple of weeks, including one just two days before she'd died.

11/3

Extreme insom, 6–7 nights/week out of bed, "mostly working," in frenzy of excitement/fear. Won't describe nature of work. Just says is consuming, expresses (humorous?) concern that she's "gone off deep end." Dismisses q re Risp (insists she just took 2 wk break due to pharm issue), says main prob is sleep, asks if cd prescribe something new. I say new med wd require in-person appt, H demurs.

11/10

Hallucinations/vivid dreams—> transformed into various figs: bird, writer, etc. Still sleeping v little. In re to my expr of concern, desire for in-person appt, becomes angry, says v impt project at work, lack of understanding from Nick, now me too, etc. Refuses to sched next phone app. Poss rec drugs? Psych break?

11/18

V gloomy, dark—> depressive ep? Apols for prior sessions, embarr, blames sleeplessness. Says doesn't need new meds, wants to handle on own. Describes stress re Nick, uncertainty re marriage, becomes incr upset, cries, distraught. "Am I making a giant mistake?" Describes terror re something she's seen (won't spec), asks (v unus) whether I've enjoyed my life—in re my saying focus ought to be on her, cries again. What abt putting off engagement, I sugg—> no firm decision nec just now, just delay. H says no, not poss, cries again. I say: clear you're in great distress. Come for in-person appt or cannot respons continue to treat. H proms to consider.

Isn't there a medieval torture device in which all the blood is let out of a person, like a bathtub being drained? This is what seemed to have happened to me by the time I put down the last page of notes. The deli's window reflected a picture of me sitting frozen with my elbows on the table, a piece of paper and an empty cup in front of me, my head in my hands. The girl who had been behind the counter was now moving quietly around the dining room, sweeping under tables with a plastic broom. For a few seconds I didn't even have any thoughts—I just sat there vibrating with the awful, empty, staggered feeling, pain in the shape of a human being. If the police had stormed in at that moment, I wouldn't have cared about being arrested—I wouldn't have cared about being shot.

But, of course, my thoughts wouldn't stay back for long—Hannah hadn't wanted to marry me. This had been the problem. This had been her secret. How many nights had I thrown my arm over her in our bed at Wright while she lay there trying not to cry? How many conversations had she spent churning with secret misery? How could she have—? How could I not have—? And did this mean she'd—? And if she had, was it really because—?

So consuming was my suffering, my feeling of having fallen into a whirlpool, that it took me a few seconds even to notice that the pink-haired girl was now standing next to me.

"Did you drop this?"

She held out a yellow post-it note covered in Dr. Blythe's writing.

Phone message from H on 11/19 @ 10:15PM
Says pls call, she has to tell me something about the Kemps, used to live in the house, papers she found in fmr director's box (sounds v scattered—manic? intox?); something happened to female Kemp; H worried could be what's happening to her.
Msg returned 9AM on 11/20. No answer.

. . .

Driving at semi-normal speeds, it takes an hour and fifteen minutes to get from the Bronx to Hibernia. I made the trip, with Dr. Blythe's notes now scattered in my lap, in just over forty minutes. The state troopers nestled behind their little hills on the Taconic had never concerned me less; slowing down on unlit, shoulder-less curves had never seemed to me more optional. My phone, in the passenger's seat beside me, showed that I'd missed half a dozen calls in the past couple of hours—at least a few of them from the Rampes—but the only responses I could muster to this news was to turn off my phone and drive faster.

It's incredible how sensitive your mind turns out to be to geographical details that you didn't even know you remembered; just the sight of the gray trees and electricity towers, the low dark mountains and wide black reservoirs, touched some nerve in me that had been left bloody and exposed since Hannah's death. The exit signs ticking by—Cold Spring, Sylvan Lake, James Baird State Park—could, for their effect on me, just as well have read: *Doomed, doomed, doomed.* My cells knew a disaster had taken place in this direction. The human animal is an obsessive and hopeless self-protector.

It's hard for me to reconstruct now what exactly I thought I was going to Hibernia to get, or to find. The box of Jim's papers, at least. Whatever it was that had made Hannah leave that last message for Dr. Blythe. But there was something more basic than that too. When I was a kid and I would lose something—my backpack, a soccer cleat—my mom would always say, in her infinite-patience voice, "Now where was the last place you know you had it?" This is maybe the most complete explanation for what I was doing: I was returning to the last place where I'd had even a slight grasp on Hannah. If she really had decided not to marry me, I needed to find the place, needed to find the moment, where it had happened.

The car, by the time I passed the exit for Poughkeepsie, had started making the ticking/flapping noise it did sometimes at high speeds, and the roadkill had taken on a forbidding, head-on-a-pike quality. There was a deer with its neck doubled back. A turkey, or anyway some sort of bird, whose feathers had arranged themselves into a fan poking straight up from the pulp of its body. I'd spent the past half hour thinking, in a desperate, banging-your-head-against-the-wall sort of way, about why Hannah hadn't called off the wedding, and about the Kemps, whose name I hadn't thought of in months. They'd lived at Wright in the 1950s, before it became a museum, and the wife had disappeared, and Butch had gone to school with one of the kids. That Hannah would have called Dr. Blythe to talk about them the night before she died—that their story could possibly have had any sort of urgent meaning for her—was so bizarre, had so little to do with any version of her last weeks I could imagine, that I thought I must have misread something. For her to have killed herself because she couldn't bear the thought of marrying me, or because she'd been gripped by her old psychological demons—these were horrible to think about, but I could at least semi-understand them. But for her to have killed herself because . . .

So that was something else that had happened, apparently: my doubts about whether Hannah had committed suicide had collapsed completely. The rest of my grieving, the rest of my life, was going to have to be conducted amidst the rubble.

Entering Hibernia—exiting the Taconic, driving past the hardware store with its lumber yard and the gas station with free air, making that swoop of a turn onto 82—was so clearly unacceptable to the instinctual parts of me that I had to physically restrain myself from making a U-turn. Part of the horror, I think, had to do with how unchanged everything was. The volunteer fire station was still standing there with its open garage and its marquee ("CALLS YTD: 216"). The farm stand was still advertising specials on chicken sausage and winter squash. The diner was still looking to hire a cook, no experience necessary. I guess I'd half-expected Hibernia to fold up its tent as soon as Hannah died. The death of an emperor is the only kind of death in which the world's response makes any sort of sense: the silent parades, the darkened houses, the weeping strangers all in black. Here my sun had fallen out of the sky, and Peck's was still selling buckets of night crawlers for $2.99.

I turned onto Culver and drove toward the museum—it was now almost six o'clock, dark in that total, Hibernia way—and as I approached, gravel and branches popping and crackling under my tires, I noticed something strange: there were cars parked along the road. Maybe half a dozen altogether, Subarus and pickup trucks and old beaten Hondas, all just in front of Wright. So not everything was exactly the way I'd left it. The lights in the first floor of the museum were on. Walking up the driveway, I thought I could hear, or maybe just feel, music coming from inside the house, like a fever through skin. No explanation I could think of made any sense. A party in memory of Hannah. An unprecedentedly successful evening event. Festive home invaders.

I walked up onto the porch, and there just inside the front door—which was unlocked—stood Donna, wearing a silver party hat and a look of cheerful welcome that dissolved the second she saw me.

"You came," she said, wrapping me in a clumsy hug.

There were maybe a dozen people scattered around the museum's foyer and kitchen area, all holding little clear plastic cups. On the welcome table there was a tray arrayed with half-wrapped Brie and a plate of crumbly cookies. All the overhead lights were on, and the feeling—jazz was playing from computer speakers in the living room—was of a not-very-successful office party. I felt, for no good reason, obscurely outraged, as if I were an adult who'd come home to find teenagers doing keg stands. One of the volunteer educators, Edna, nodded at me from over by the wood stove—she was sipping a beer and gesticulating to a woman in a tan baseball cap. The Wrighters stood clustered by the Wright family portrait in the living room, dribbling crumbs and providing a good three-quarters of the party's animation ("He hadn't even *read* her!" I heard the Viking type bark). A bearded man I didn't recognize was taking a picture of one of the wall signs with his iPhone.

Donna pulled me toward Hannah's old office, under the stairs. "How are you doing?" she said. "I mean, I can imagine how you must be doing, but I can't believe you came all this way. I hope you didn't feel like you had to or anything."

"I don't know what you're talking about," I said. She went on exactly as if I hadn't spoken.

"Well, we sure appreciate you being here. You look pretty roughed up. Not that you look bad. Not that you shouldn't look bad. But—can I get you some cider? Or wine? I wanted to be at the funeral, I was going to be, I heard it was a beautiful service, but then my dad fell, broke his pelvis, now he's on painkillers, which the doctor says is usually the beginning of the end for somebody his age, he's ninety-two, even though this same doctor said it was the end of the end when he had pneumonia like two years ago, so … Anyway, Jesus. Twenty-five years, huh? I guess it makes sense, but it still breaks your heart, doesn't it? All our work, mothballed. Board didn't even give a reason, just *effective immediately*, all that kind of stuff. And I wanted to say, Hey, Hannah loved this place, you wanna honor her? Try keeping it open. I know that's how you feel too. But of course as soon as they announce it, there go all your school groups, there go all your funders. You sure I can't get you something to drink?"

So that's what this gathering was—the closing party for the museum. The board had voted a week after Hannah's death, it turned out. That Monday had been the Wright House's last day open to the public. Donna said she'd emailed me an invitation, or tried to ("Paperless Post keeps telling me my profile needs updating, but I don't *want* a profile, I just want to—"), and maybe someone had sent me the news about the closing too.

"The thing I hate to think is, here's going to be this whole generation of kids who don't even know Wright's name," Donna said. I just nodded, looking down. She seemed nervous in a way I'd never seen her—eyes flitting around, sipping at her empty cup. So not even someone as socially oblivious as Donna could help acting uncomfortable around the boyfriend of the late Hannah Rampe.

"I'm actually not going to stay," I said. "I just came to pick up a couple of Hannah's things. Is our room open?"

"Oh, hey, I meant to write you about that, I took most of you guys' stuff back to my house, figured it was safer there and then I could just ship it down to you or whatever. Didn't want, you know, looky lous coming by and peeking in the windows. Plus we've got so much space, since we cleaned up, it wasn't really—"

"Maybe I could just go by and pick them up."

"Yeah, definitely after the party we can do that. I'll take you over. Wait, did you say hi to Butch? I know he's been dying to talk to you. *Hey, Butch!* You said you didn't want any wine, right?"

Butch, in his tan shirt and jeans, walked over and crushed my hand feelingly.

"How you holding up?"

"Well . . ."

So now I was a guest at the Wright House party. I hadn't eaten all day, I realized, which might go some way toward explaining the floaty feeling that was building in me. I ate a few of the crumbly cookies, which turned out to have been made from one of Sarah Wright's recipes, heavy on fennel seed. I drank red wine that made my mouth feel like decaying copper. I stood at the base of the stairs and listened to a woman I didn't know, and who didn't seem to know who I was, explain why she wouldn't be able to get her felting machine fixed until March, and how this meant disappointed customers up and down the Hudson Valley.

At some point I found myself in the living room, standing by the knotty mantel with the Wrighters. "We'd love to induct Hannah into the society posthumously, if that's all right," said Barry, the leader. "It's so rare to meet someone who comes into a new place and gets what it's about right away."

"You could tell she was just such a *kind* person," said the female Wrighter, Annie, who wasn't wearing a bra and whose hair was pulled into a single gray braid with a binder clip holding the end. I looked away for a second, and when I looked back I was surprised to see tears in her eyes. "And you seem so kind too. I know we didn't get to spend very much time together, but just in that little bit I always got the feeling that the two of you . . ."

The Viking, Todd—who was one of those tall people who conducts his entire life stooping—wrapped his arm around me and guided me toward the window that looked out on the firewood heap. I could feel the cold coming off the glass. Todd was in his forties, with bushy eyebrows and a wide, angular, shield-shaped face. He was wearing loose corduroy pants and a gray sweater whose cuffs he kept pushing up his forearms.

"I just wanted to talk to you real quick," he said. He was tense. He had, even when he was speaking quietly, the sort of resonant voice you can feel in your skull. By this point I'd finished my fourth or fifth cup of wine, and my stomach had started shifting. "I lost my sister when I was ten, okay?" he said. "A heart thing. So I get what you're feeling. I know you don't even feel like you're really here. I get how the only real person is her. I get that." I assumed that this was the thing he wanted to say, the thing he'd been nervous about sharing, so I made some appreciative noises, but now he looked over his shoulder and stooped even lower. "Look. Hannah didn't die by accident, okay? And it wasn't because she was depressed. You know that. People who live here ... It's this fucking *place*. She found something out. You didn't come up here to get your sweatshirts. You want to know what she saw. Remember: buried, not burned. You're the closest of any of us."

Barry appeared behind us and said, over-heartily, "How are you two doing for wine?"

"We're just fine, Captain," Todd said, speaking in his public-consumption voice again. The rest of the Wrighters had drifted over toward me and Todd, and now they re-formed a loose circle around us. My surface temperature had dropped precipitously. Everyone seemed to be waiting for someone else to think of what to say. "Nick, where are you staying tonight?" Annie said, finally. "You aren't driving back to the city, I hope?"

"I'm not sure," I said. "I—excuse me."

I hurried, in the way of people who have suddenly realized they might vomit, through the living room and kitchen exhibit and back into the caretaker's apartment. The door was open after all. Our bathroom was empty now—towels gone from the hangers, Hannah's loofah gone from the shower—and for a few minutes I stood hunched over the toilet, willing myself to retch. Todd's words, plus some critical mass of wine, had put my entire system into a state of three-alarm emergency. My heart was racing, my legs were tingling. I felt seconds from either passing out or throwing up—they were expressions of the same impulse. But neither one happened, so I splashed my face with cold water and stood breathing heavily for a minute in the middle of the last room where Hannah and I had lived.

It really had been stripped. The room reminded me now, even more than when we'd first moved in, of a lonely and unwell man's apartment. There was our double bed, now a bare mattress on a box spring. There was the round red and orange rug, faded and dust-fuzzed. There were our cracked-pane windows, now acting as pitch-black mirrors. I sat down in the old chair by the window—a heavy wooden chair with wonky wheels—and spun myself around so I was facing the plywood shelf above the desk. Here, slump-spined and yellow-speckled, were the half-dozen books that someone had at some point decided it was crucial for any Wright House caretaker to own. *A People's History of Hibernia. The Selected Letters of Edmund Wright. Hibernia Town Directory. The Selected Journals of Edmund Wright. Native Plants and Wildflowers of the Northeast.* I don't think I'd ever touched a single one of these books, but I'd occasionally seen one or another of them on Hannah's bedside table.

I was in no hurry to return to the party, so I finished what was left in my cup, then pulled out *The Selected Letters*—an extremely self-published-looking blue-green paperback—and cracked it open to a middle page. Here was Edmund Wright in the spring of 1868, apologizing to someone for being too long out of touch. *Having not written to you in some months, the task acquired perhaps exaggerated difficulty in my mind, since there had accumulated so many equally significant pieces of news that to choose among them seemed to require a prodigious act of winnowing.* And here he was, twenty pages later, writing about *a whiskered gentleman pausing to sneeze in the middle of the road* and how the sight had reminded him of a study he'd meant to conduct about *the peculiar class of bodily acts that are neither wholly voluntary nor wholly automatic.*

How was it—the thought came to me as another, sharper sort of pain in my stomach—that the course of Hannah's life, and the course of my life, had been shaped by this babbling white-bearded man? I stared at his tea-colored picture in its oval on the cover, like a photo in a locket. Deep eye wrinkles, tufty side-burns, long earlobes. I'd never really thought about Edmund Wright the person in the months when we'd been living there—he'd been half a storybook character to me, like the faces on dollar bills—but now, somehow, in the dim weird loneliness of that room, downstairs from where he and his family had slept, Wright became real to me. He'd dug crust out of the corners of his eyes, he'd looked up from his desk and wondered if he should take a walk before dinner, he'd burped and been surprised by the smell. Edmund Wright had lived, and so Hannah had died. There were more steps to it than that, I knew—including the Kemps, including me—but right then it felt as simple as a light switch: down, off.

I didn't notice that Butch was standing in the doorway until he spoke. "Didn't realize you were back here," he said. "I'm sup-posed to be locking up. Party's winding down."

I nodded, stood up, slid Wright's letters back onto the shelf.

"Have you seen Donna?" I said. For some reason my voice came out as a croak.

"What's that, bud?"

"Do you know where Donna is? I was supposed to leave with her, get some stuff from her house."

"Sorry," he said, walking over to turn off the light in the bathroom. "She took off about ten minutes ago. You need a ride somewhere? She ran out of here like something was chasing her."

． ． ．

I'd only ever been to Donna's house once before—her car had died, one afternoon not long after we'd moved into the museum, and I'd still been in my good-natured rural neighbor mode then. A few miles down 82, I remembered, and then a left, or possibly a right, on . . . Hobb's Lane? Bull's Head Road? It was a one-story brick house, I knew, that she lived in with her sister, and it had a steep uneven driveway. In the dark I couldn't read the street signs until I was almost past them. Here, lit up in my headlights like a safari animal, was a house with a yellow VW out front. Here was a house with a massive above-ground pool. Here was a stretch of dark, vine-tangled woods with a row of No Trespassing signs planted along the edge.

It took me about half an hour of meandering to finally find Donna's street—I remembered her explaining to me that the man who lived in this log cabin on the corner had inherited a million dollars from his uncle but had decided to stay right here in Hibernia because that's who he was. Rusty metal sunflowers stood tilting in Donna's lawn, marking out the flagstone path leading to her front door. Her mailbox was open. Her car with its cracked windshield and bumper stickers ("HISTORIC PRESERVATIONISTS MAKE IT LAST LONGER") was parked at an angle in the driveway. The shades in the house's front windows were down, and, so far as I could tell, every light except for the porch light was off. It was as if she'd raced home and leapt directly under the covers.

One of the little-discussed benefits of grief—especially

grief supplemented by slight drunkenness—is that it frees you up from most social norms. I walked up to the front door and pressed the doorbell a half-dozen times, listening to each ring fade inside the house. Maybe she really wasn't home, I thought. Maybe her sister—what was her name? Celia?—had driven them to Uncle Sonny's, where they were now polishing off a slab of chocolate cake. I pressed my forehead to the window to the right of the front door, and got a glimpse of a small dark kitchen with checked floors. I rang the bell a few more times, then walked back to the driveway and, not sure what I was expecting to see, peered into Donna's car (a roll of paper towels, an empty Tupperware container).

It just so happened, though, that this, standing on the right side of her car, placed me at the ideal angle—if I'd still been at the front door I would have missed it—to see a tiny gap open and close in the Venetian blinds over one of the windows on the right side of the house. Someone peeking out, shining a tiny light, and then disappearing.

I walked straight to the window—the yard sloped down on that side of the house, but I could still reach the window by standing on my toes—and I rapped my knuckles against the glass. The blinds didn't budge, so I shouted, *"Donna! It's Nick!"* (This, incidentally—hearing my own voice—was when I realized how much I must have sounded, to her neighbors, like a belligerent, drunken burglar, and how possible it was that I would at any moment be shot.) *"You left without me! I need to get Hannah's papers!"*

There was still no movement inside, so I walked back around to the front of the house and up to the door. *"I know you're home!"* I called, pressing the bell. *"I need to get my stuff!"* I was by this point alternating between bell rings and fist thumps, and I was just reaching to ring the bell for the fourth or fifth time when the door cracked open.

Donna's sister, who I realized I'd never actually laid eyes on, appeared in the doorway—a four-inch sliver of her, anyway. She had a shriveled-apple face and she wore a green plaid robe; she looked like Donna if Donna had spent a couple of years sick in bed. Her expression was less outraged than startled. A light was on in the hall behind her. I explained to her, in my best *Who was doing all that shouting?* voice, who I was and what I was doing there. It was not lost on some part of me that I might not, in having forced a seventy-year-old woman to come to her door at ten o'clock at night, be entirely in the right.

"I'm sorry," she whispered. "Donna's having a migraine, she came home and went straight to bed. I think it'd be better if you came back tomorrow."

"I just need to get Hannah's things."

"I'm sorry, but that can't happen tonight," she said.

"I'm not staying in Hibernia—I need to get them now. I won't bother Donna. Please."

"I'm sorry," she said. Her voice had become harder, the door gap narrower. "I'll make sure Donna calls you when she's feeling better."

She moved to close the door then, and what I did in response was subtle—much subtler than she would later make it sound. What I did was I edged the front of my shoe into the crack of the door—a move honed by countless nearly missed Q trains—and slowly leveraged it open. That's all. There was no striking, no pushing, no forced entry.

"I just want to come in for a minute," I said, my foot still bracing the door.

"You need to get back in your car," she said.

She was, I noticed, standing as if she had an interest not just in having the door closed but also in keeping me from seeing whatever was behind her. So I leaned around to peer past her, and before she could stop me—she shifted like a mime—I got a glimpse down the house's carpeted central hallway, at the far end of which knelt Donna, still dressed in her sweater from the party, rummaging through a cardboard box.

This was when I actually did force my way inside, though in fairness, Donna's sister had by this point largely stopped holding the door. I stopped at the key table; Donna looked up at me with a blank, scared expression. "How's your migraine?" I said.

"I'm feeling better," she said, scrambling to her feet. She stood in front of the box.

"That's Hannah's box."

"I was just looking through some stuff here, and most of the papers aren't even hers. They're the museum's. I can give you some of it, but it's going to take me a while to sort out what's what. Like I said, I can mail it down to you in the city, or you can come back sometime when—"

"Why won't you just give it to me?"

"I just want to make sure that whatever's in there is actually stuff that—"

"What happened to Jan Kemp?" I hadn't known I was going to say this. The effect on Donna was as if I'd struck her between the eyes with a pebble.

"I don't know what you're talking about."

I took a few steps closer. "Jan Kemp. She used to live at Wright. What happened to her?" My voice had gotten quieter. Donna's sister had disappeared into some other part of the house.

"How the hell am I supposed to know? Go ask, you know, go ask some bozo down at Peck's, they'll tell you Bigfoot took her, what difference does it make?"

"Tell me what happened."

"I wasn't there, for Christ's sakes," she said. There was panic in her eyes. "Look, I'm sorry as hell for what you're going through, but I can't stand here in the middle of the night talking about every crazy goddamn idea in your head. You already woke up Delia, now you're—"

"What happened to Jan Kemp?"

"Look, I don't know how many times you want me to repeat myself, but—"

She stopped talking. Humans don't cock their heads at weird noises the way dogs do, but right then we both did a pretty good approximation. Sirens are a rare sound in Hibernia.

I used to think of myself as preternaturally self-possessed, a man without a breaking point. I'd see people melt down after some succession of stresses—bad day at work, stalled train, lost set of keys—and I'd think, *How fragile*. But we're all fragile; some of us just take slightly more shaking to break.

This is a long way of saying that I'm not proud of what I did next. I body-checked Donna a few inches to the side (she stayed on her feet but hit the wall) and I blindly grabbed a few folded pages from the top of the box. Then, while Donna shouted, "That's a fucking *assault*, is what that is!," I raced out the front door and down the driveway and leapt back in the Volvo. The sirens sounded closer, but I still couldn't see any lights. I reversed too fast and took off, with a squeal of tires that was more of a shriek, in the opposite direction from the way I'd come. This, I thought, stuffing the pages into my jacket pocket, must be how cars end up in ditches on their backs.

I'd never driven this far on Hobb's Lane, and for all I knew the road would dead-end, but it didn't, it just rolled on and on past white farm fences, through tunnels of dead trees, past pitch-black houses. I saw a sliver of moon behind somebody's barn. I thought I might have seen a coyote stepping out of a dark tangle of bushes. I was burbling, nonsense-praying to myself, speeding along the middle of the road fast enough that I didn't have enough spare attention to check the speedometer. The shock of the siren had scared the tipsiness right out of me. Well, *almost* right out of me. So long as I tilted my body with each curve, I felt in pretty good control. The wheel was cold. The air blowing from the heater smelled like burning plastic. The world outside the circle of my headlights was entirely black—road, fields, sky, one undifferentiated backdrop. Silver tree trunks kept appearing, signaling where the road curved, inviting me to crash into them.

But I didn't crash, and I didn't see any other cars, and I couldn't hear the siren anymore, although sometimes I thought maybe it was faintly there inside the ringing in my ears. *Hannah I don't know what I'm doing I'm making so many mistakes please help me God I'm so sorry please.* I was conducting the first successful high-speed escape in history. Or maybe the police hadn't been coming for me at all and so I was conducting a needless high-speed drive in a random direction. Now I was climbing a hill, passing a house with a twinkling lawn village of Christmas lights; now I was racing down the other side of the hill, through blackness so total I held my breath. I felt like I was playing a too-hard video game, one that would send me flying off into un-drawn space at any moment. I was coming around a curve at the bottom of the hill, having the thought that maybe my entire life could be managed by imagining that it was a video game, that the obstacles were deliberate and the goals were attainable and the puzzles were solvable—when I realized that there was a spaceship immediately behind me. A blaze of red and blue lights filling all of my mirrors. The sirens didn't come on until a second later, for some reason, the sound dopplering up and then pouncing on me, filling my legs, my chest, my head. I pulled over by nearly crashing into a high fence. My hands were quaking against the wheel. I was breathing so hard that I thought my lungs might pop. I heard shouting and slamming doors and I saw shadows racing toward me and I knew, before Sheriff Cole's face appeared above me, before the whole thing dissolved into noise and shoving and flashing lights, that here it was, finally— the punishment I'd been racing toward.

[Edmund Wright's journal]

Dec. 1

… What a self-important old fool I've been! It was not I who was becoming more practiced at sustaining the episodes of inhabitation; it was the spirits who were becoming practiced at inhabiting me; it was they who longed to remain, gaining ever greater mastery of my mind & senses, until they could besiege me with the vision that would suit their ends.

In my student days I read of a species of caterpillar that was prone to a most frightful misfortune. This sorry caterpillar would on occasion be attacked by a small & vicious wasp who, in the course of his assault, would lay a great many eggs in the caterpillar's abdomen. The wasp's eggs would then proceed, by some chemical means, to control the caterpillar's movements, inducing it to gather precisely the type of nutriment they craved. Once the eggs had matured sufficiently, they would come pouring forth from the caterpillar's underbelly, a hellish horde …

Thus do I, at the end of my researches, having spent all the fall playing host to spirits, find myself husked & destroyed …

[Admittance materials, Northern Dutchess Hospital]

Welcome to Sommers 11 North, a 26-bed acute care psychiatric unit, where your friend or family member has been admitted.

Visiting hours are daily, from 11:00AM to 4:30PM, **except on Tuesdays between 12PM and 2PM,** when all patients are required to attend Community Meeting.

The next business day following the admission of your friend or family member, a social worker will be available between the hours of 11AM and 1PM to meet with you. If you cannot make this session, a social worker will contact you to schedule an alternative time.

Please contact Dr. Gutman (see Staff Directory, page 2) immediately if your friend or family member expresses the idea of hurting himself/herself, hurting someone else, or running away from the hospital. If Dr. Gutman is unavailable, please ask to speak with the charge nurse or her/his designee and state that you have urgent patient information that must be acted upon immediately.

. . .

4

One of the staples of my fantasy life, when I was at the height of my musical ambitions/delusions, was the speech I'd give when I won my first major award. Sometimes this speech took place in a ballroom where everybody looked up at me from round tables, setting down their silverware in charmed amazement. Sometimes it took place in an actual Grammy-style theater, where I jogged down the aisle and up the stage stairs smiling in friendly fake surprise. A standard feature of these imaginary speeches, anyway, was that they contained a brief section on feeling humbled—how, while it might seem as if this were a moment for maximal ego inflation, this whole award-receiving experience had actually only made me more appreciative than ever of all the people whose help I couldn't have accomplished this without and of just how much there still was for me to learn.

I would now support a constitutional amendment ordering anyone who claims to be humbled in this way to be transferred immediately to the fourth-floor Sommers Psychiatric Ward at Northern Dutchess Hospital. To be humbled is to wake up wearing an un-tearable plastic bracelet with your name on it; to find out you'll have to earn "positive behavior points" in order to buy Combos from the vending machine; to sleep in a salmon-sheeted twin bed five feet from a fortysomething stranger who cracks his knuckles and farts poisonously in his sleep.

The specifics of how I came to enter the hospital are both

tedious and depressing, so I won't go too much into them except to say that if Sheriff Cole hadn't been in the car that pulled me over, and if it hadn't been for the understanding of Dutchess County Second District Judge Marilyn Everts—who, perfectly reasonably, deemed me a danger to myself—I would have ended up somewhere worse.

The hospital was half an hour north of Hibernia, a big gloomy campus of duck-less ponds and half-empty parking lots. The buildings—there were three or four of them—were painted yellow and looked like haphazardly constructed college dorms, rows of windows and sliding-glass front doors. My first thought, pulling in, was that it resembled the conference center in Connecticut where I'd once spent an ill-advised weekend listening to presentations about digital marketing for artists and entrepreneurs.

Checking in—that first morning of forms and information sessions and intake interviews—was a bizarre, bleak, indoctrination-type experience. Complicated Grief Disorder, people kept impressing on me, is a diagnosable condition. What I'd been going through, they insisted, didn't have to do with Dr. Blythe's notes, or Donna's lies, or any cardboard box; this was grief, this was shock, this was despair, this was just how these things felt. I'd been, they said, the victim of a series of delusions. I shouldn't be thinking about Hannah's death while I was hospitalized, shouldn't be trying to solve anything. My only job was to take my pills, to do the various therapies, and to wait for my mind's vital signs to stabilize. I was, in other words, supposed to accept not just that I'd lost Hannah; I'd also gone some ways toward losing my mind.

The main thing that struck me those first few days—the thing other than the place's incredible, soul-corroding grimness—was how hard life was for the patients there, and how little there seemed to be that anyone could do about it. It would happen sometimes that a group of trainee nurses or a few administrators from another hospital would sit in on a group, and the difference between the civilians in the room and the patients would be as stark and essential as the difference between a lightbulb that's on and one that's off. Something was gone from the patients at Sommers: some flavor, some force. Life for the non-patients was full of gossip, interest, jokes, projects that might or might not come through—life for the patients was an ordeal to be suffered through (or, if they could find the means, not suffered through). It terrified me to realize that I'd somehow slipped from the first category of person into the second.

I had plenty of time for this kind of reflection. You know those intervals in life when your plane has been delayed five hours and you've already finished your book, or you're stuck in traffic so bad that you might as well turn the car off? Life in a psychiatric hospital, assuming you're well enough to retain any sense of time at all, is one of those intervals stretched out to fill every minute.

I was, as a 5150, supposed to spend seven weeks at Sommers—this dictated the wing I was placed in and the privileges I was allowed (visitors, yes; day trips, no). Both of my parents came to see me, in that first week, and their stated position—I suspected they'd been prepped by a social worker—was that I was doing the right thing, I was in exactly the right place, that all they cared about was me getting well. But they looked, both of them, as if they'd found me living in a dumpster. It had only been a couple of weeks since I'd last seen them, and *Jesus, Nick, what happened?* was flashing on both of their faces. I'd lost weight. I hadn't shaved. I was wearing plaid pajama pants Sheriff Cole had bought for me. I must, in other words, have appeared to them just as horrifying as my fellow patients had initially appeared to me. When they left at the end of the hour—there was a whole complicated system of sign-in desks and doors that needed to be buzzed—I felt the gruesome adult equivalent of what I'd felt when they'd dropped me off at summer camp; these strangers are now my people.

My roommate—our door was never allowed to be fully closed—was a man named Diego. Our bedroom was tile-floored, white-walled, anonymous in the way of rooms that see many unwell inhabitants. Diego was in the hospital because of a fight he'd had at his last job, at an auto shop in Poughkeepsie. I couldn't get all the details—he spoke in bursts of vividness that didn't quite link up—but there had been a pair of jumper cables, an arrogant college boy, a call to the police. Diego's diagnosis of his own mental condition was: "I get sometimes so my thoughts don't make no sense." He had a short black ponytail and a bottomless supply of eucalyptus cough drops, and, because he'd been hospitalized twice before, he acted as my mentor.

"This is Linda. Good lady, born in Nebraska or someplace. Her husband, normal dude, they're married for like twenty years, turns out he's gay plus a crackhead, and he's emptying her bank account. One day she goes to get money so she can take her mother to the doctor, finds out she doesn't even own her house anymore.

"Over by the window, that's Steve. Twenty-two years old, tried to kill himself last year with the cord from a air conditioner, 'cept the cord snapped, dude fell broke both his feet. I got no beef with him, but some other dudes, they don't like the way he looks at people in group.

"This is Eileen. *How you doin', sweetheart?* She don't eat. She went one whole year before she came in here, didn't eat nothing but water and five pieces of popcorn a day. Now they got her with tubes.

"Who else. Oh, that's the professor. We call him that 'cause he just sits around all day and reads. He don't even care what, dude would read a cereal box. I seen him do better on *Jeopardy* than the guys who make forty thousand. *Hey professor, how many rivers are in Africa? How many legs do ants have?*"

There was, in other words, enough collective suffering at Sommers to dissolve any of our individual misfortunes. After a week or so, my story—dead girlfriend, delusions, drunken car chase—became just another drop in the endless gray ocean. I would hear myself saying things like "And so I broke in and stole her notes," and, "I found out she'd been thinking about breaking up with me when she died," and the other people in the circle would just nod, sigh, say yeah, they'd had cousins who'd gone through things like that.

Every Tuesday morning at 10:30 we had a Coping Skills group. Each week's session focused on a different patient, and my first week there was Diego's turn. He was telling the story of a fight he'd had with his sister's boyfriend.

"Okay," Dr. Mital said. "Okay." Dr. Mital was a young Indian woman with dramatic eye makeup and an engagement ring. "Do you know what your thoughts were, when he pushed you?"

"I was thinking *What the fuck you do that for, I'm gonna cut you.*"

"Okay. So"—reaching over to write illegibly on her whiteboard—"*What the blank did you do that for, I want to cut you.* Is that accurate?"

"Yeah that's it."

"And your feelings were anger, I think we can say. Would you say there was some fear in there?"

"I wasn't afraid of shit. *He* was afraid."

"Okay so anger. Maybe some annoyance? Is that fair to say? And on an intensity scale, how would you rate these feelings? How angry were you?"

"Ooh, way up here. Like about to blow."

"Should we say a seven or an eight? Now, let's bring in the group and talk about some skillful things you could have done when you were feeling anger at a seven or an eight."

"He could have breathed?" Eileen said breathily.

"He could have bashed the guy in the teeth with his bike lock," Steve muttered.

"Okay so let's talk about whether that would have been skillful. How do we define skillfulness, in this context?"

"Effectively meeting our goals and values."

"And what are our goals and values in this situation?"

Diego said, "Not going to jail."

"Not going to jail. That's a good goal. Any others?"

"Not being the kind of dude who has to jack people when they get in his face?"

"Nonviolence? Is that the value you're describing?"

"Yeah. Nonviolence. Other people can be getting all wild on you and you just say, *Uh-uh, you ain't even worth one drop of blood.*"

"And can anyone think of a behavior that might have served these goals and values? Not going to jail and nonviolence?"

No one said anything for a minute or two—these sessions, because of overmedication or just the strangeness of hospital culture, always contained long pockets of silence—and then for the first time since I'd been there, the professor raised his hand. "Would you mind if I went and found Nurse Carol?" he said. "I'm having an issue with my blood sugar. My cereal ran out at breakfast, and the only bananas they had were mush." He talked with his hands by his mouth, rubbing his cheek through his beard. His notebook was bouncing in his lap.

"Go ahead, James," Dr. Mital said.

The professor hurried out of the room, shaking his head as if to dislodge a fly. Diego, turning around in his chair, called out through the door, "What, my story's not smart enough for you?"

. . .

Tuesdays and Thursdays I had individual counseling with Dr. Mital in the B Hall. We met in one of the glass-walled rooms across from the TV area (most rooms at Sommers were glass-walled, in keeping with the student center/panopticon vibe). We sat across a little round table from each other, close enough that I would sometimes accidentally bump her when I rearranged my legs. She wore her pantsuit, I wore my pajamas. A year ago, I'd think, she and I could have been colleagues meeting to plan a holiday party; now she was keeping one eye on the emergency button.

Dr. Mital had told me in our first session that one of our main progress goals was going to be coming up with a "good-enough story" of Hannah's death. "Most traumatic deaths," she said, "are, to some extent, mysteries." (I rubbed Hannah's papers in my pocket, the pages now as soft as the fabric of my pajamas.) "Survivors often find it more comfortable, emotionally, to focus on 'solving' the mystery—even if this activity is actually very unpleasant—rather than on facing whatever feelings they're having. So we're going to do our best to come up with a story that stays within the bounds of what we know, and then we're going to practice saying, *Good enough.*"

The story we came up with, over a handful of dry-mouthed, silence-punctuated sessions, was: I had been engaged to a woman with a history of mental instability, and the stresses of thinking about marriage, plus a new job and living situation, plus some unwise decisions about her medicine, had pushed her into a crisis. *(This is good so far, Nick, you're doing great. I like that word* crisis. *Keep going.)* And so one morning in November ... What about the things Hannah had told Dr. Blythe about the Kemps? *(Well, she was clearly in great distress. Can you bring in experience from your own life? Does your thinking become more or less clear when you're extremely upset?)* And so one morning in November, although we couldn't know with a hundred percent certainty if it had been an accident *(Yes, good. One hundred percent certainty is one hundred percent impossible),* Hannah had gone out and walked into the river. What about the canoe, though? *(Let's not get hung up on that. This might be one of those details that we'll never fully understand.)* And she'd drowned, whether or not she'd meant to *(Good, yes)* and ... What about her not leaving a note? *(More than half of all suicides don't leave notes. Let's try not to speculate.)* And we'd found her body that afternoon, much too late to do any good, and the downward-spiral portion of my life *(Can we rephrase that less judgmentally?)*—the recent difficult portion of my life—had begun.

So, this was the patchy and unsatisfying version of events that it was now my job to accept. Whenever I found myself disappearing down a mental alleyway—whenever I found myself reading and rereading the list in my pocket, wondering what Hannah had meant—I was supposed to check in by focusing for thirty seconds on the sensations in my feet, and then I was supposed to consult what Dr. Mital and I had written together in my notebook. The words *Kemp* and *canoe* and *Donna* and *Wrighters* were all supposed to act as warning bells now, indicators that my thoughts had drifted off into the unverifiable. I could—with the help of diaphragmatic breathing—make room for the uncomfortable thoughts and feelings, but I didn't have to follow them.

This all sounds culty and soft-headed, as I write it out, but the truth is that I was sufficiently desperate for relief, and sufficiently skeptical of my own judgment, that I actually signed on to Dr. Mital's approach, most of the time. Hannah had died because some people's brain chemistry predisposes them to acts of self-destruction, and all the stories I'd been telling were clouds of fog around that simple fact. Go through anyone's papers after they die and you'll find fifty things that don't add up, rabbit holes you could fall down. All but a tiny slice of the things that have ever happened, even to the people we love, we will never know about or understand.

So this was how I spent my time: feeling my feet, battling my brain, taking turns labeling one or another of the voices in my head as unreliable. And life in the hospital—medicated, joyless, airless—churned on. The institutional HVAC system roared and fell silent. Pancakes appeared and went cold in the cafeteria. I got used to the outside existing for me only as a series of brown-grass-and-pavement landscapes seen through sealed windows. Needing to wait for a staff member to swipe an ID card in order to get from one hallway to another no longer felt remarkable. At some point I'd even stopped noticing the slowness of everything—my inner settings had adjusted such that this was just life's tempo. I had group counseling and individual counseling. Creative Arts Therapy. CBT for Distress Tolerance. Relapse Prevention. Ask the Doctor. Roles & Relationships. I was back in college, it occurred to me—a very un-prestigious college—only this time I was majoring in Life.

And one of my main professors, appropriately, was turning out to be the professor, James. He wasn't the patient I liked best—that was probably Linda, the heartbroken Nebraskan—but he was the one most capable of complex conversation, which acted as a vitality drip for me. At some point a ritual had evolved where he and I and a couple of other patients would gather, every afternoon, in the corner of the lounge farthest from the TV. (The TV—usually tuned to the Game Show Network—

played incessantly, pitched so that you couldn't quite hear it if you wanted to and couldn't quite ignore it if you didn't want to.) The lounge was carpeted, with heavy wooden tables and waxy potted plants. The chairs and couches had square cushions covered in scratchy red fabric. There were lines of masking tape on the floor, to mark off the areas where we weren't allowed to go. This was our salon.

The professor, who I would have guessed was in his late fifties, liked to sit in the chair closest to the radiator. He'd set down whatever book he happened to be reading—once it was *The Count of Monte Cristo*, another time it was *Rich Dad Poor Dad*—and he would talk with me and Linda, or me and Diego, about whatever was going through his mind. He had crooked yellow teeth, and eyes that drooped in red-rimmed yolk sacks. He wore visibly stained khaki pants and too-big sweatshirts. He had a gray beard that covered his face about as completely as leg hair covers a leg. He looked, honestly, like someone who masturbates in the bathroom of Port Authority.

But he wasn't a pervert; he just wanted to talk. And then, just at the point when you thought he had to be winding down, he wanted to talk some more (for the pathological blatherer, the catatonically depressed are an ideal audience). Among the things he wanted to talk about: his exercise regimen. He didn't understand why people spent all this money on fancy gyms when you could just do what he did. A few squats, a couple of jumping jacks, a handful of those whatdoyoucallits with your arms, you were all set for the day. He also didn't understand how anyone could fail to see the war that was coming. Ice caps melt, here come new shipping routes, here come the Russian tankers, here comes Obama surrendering to everyone who comes into his field of vision.

Why exactly the professor had been hospitalized was a subject he steered around—a new patient, a schizophrenic woman named Marianne, asked him point-blank one afternoon and he just sneered at her before going on about oil prices. He made occasional allusions to some sort of betrayal, and to a daughter who, whenever she visited, failed to bring him the right sort of snack bars, but that was as far as he went. He showed no interest in anyone else's stories—he didn't even come to group therapy, most times; he kept the same kind of haughty curtain drawn around his life that the doctors did.

Most of the patients didn't seem to mind this; oracles are meant to be inscrutable. "What do you think," Diego asked him one day, "about Bloomberg? How come the dude got so rich but we still got people can't even fit in the shelters?"

(The professor rocked in his chair, then gave a long answer involving the Bilderberg Group.)

"Why can't we just suck pollution out of the air with a giant vacuum?" asked Linda. "You put it on the floor and all the dirt comes up. Why can't you just point it up to the sky?"

(You had to understand about solenoid valves and bio-aerosols, the professor explained.)

I, though, because of genuine curiosity or an inkling I didn't understand, couldn't leave the question of what he was doing here alone. I knew I wouldn't be able to get at it directly, so instead I developed a game of trying to bait him into revealing more about himself than he meant to. Boy did I know a thing or two about not being able to trust people, I'd suggest. Or: a guy as smart as him, he must have gone to a pretty good school; today colleges were just diploma factories, of course, but back when he went it must have been different, right? But his river of talk was not to be diverted.

My guess, if you'd asked me—and this is maybe part of why I was so interested—was that he'd done something violent. He'd once referred to Vietnam in a way that made me think he'd fought there, and he had the kind of shlubbiness-plus-self-regard that made it easy to picture him plotting against his superiors, being convinced that he alone was defending some important truth. I'd seen him once lose his temper with one of the social workers—red-faced, nostrils flared, thumping his fist against the shatterproof glass. I could imagine him in a standoff at an office complex, or standing with a butcher's knife over his bloodied boss. Dr. Mital was right—exploring a mystery, however remote, was infinitely more appealing than dwelling on how I felt.

And then one afternoon—the professor and I were the only ones in the lounge, both sipping cups of lukewarm coffee—he diverted the river for me. I don't know exactly what I'd said to bring this about; he may just have come to the mistaken conclusion, after all these conversations, that I was someone he could trust.

"I usually don't get into the story of why I'm here," he said.

(Of course not, I said, leaning forward.)

"It's the kind of thing where, you give somebody the littlest bit of an idea, they go running off to the nurses, next thing you know you're doped up on Seroquel, can barely string a sentence together. I'm working on a memoir. Memoir slash treatise. Major interest from a couple of places. Stuff already in the works. So I can't have, you know, Diego going around telling everybody my story."

(No need to explain to me about effing Diego. Please.)

"But I'll tell you a little about it, you seem like the literary type. Have you read much spiritualism? About metempsychosis? Maybe Piper? That's how I see my book. If I can get the public to actually take a look at this stuff, really understand what I'm saying, then I'm not going to be *in* a hospital, I'm going to have my name *on* a hospital, if you get what I'm saying. Major league sales potential, if I get the time to actually write the thing."

(So the book's about stuff you've experienced, then, or is it more...?)

"The place where I used to work—I can't tell you, because you better believe I'm suing their asses—anyway, where I used to work, they should have welcomed this kind of stuff. They should have been shouting it from the rooftops. Could have been their book. But instead you've got people calling my phone in the middle of the night, you've got people telling me I'm neglecting my duties, planting viruses on my computer. It's exactly the same thing I was telling you about with the Navy, how you get an institution so devoted to protecting itself that it forgets why it..."

And this, for whatever reason, was the moment when the coin finally dropped into my mental slot. The sensation was more like getting a joke than like learning a fact. So this was why I'd been drawn to the professor; this was why I'd spent all these hours peering at him, listening to him, pondering him. Some part of me—the part that ran my mind's filing system, deep in the subbasement—must have recognized him all along.

"You didn't used to work at a historic house museum, did you?" I said.

He was, for the first time since I'd met him, struck dumb. I pulled Hannah's papers out of my pocket and started to unfold them.

"Who wrote this?" he finally said, looking them over. "Your girlfriend wrote this?"

James. Jim. So now I'd met the Wright House's previous caretaker.

. . .

Jim told me his story—far less cogently than I'm going to recount it here—over a series of coffee-addled afternoons in the lounge. Sometimes he'd talk for an hour without a break; sometimes he'd stop after just a few minutes, muttering about a headache, and spend the rest of the afternoon staring out into the hospital courtyard. I continued, on those days, to see Dr. Mital, to sit mouthing platitudes in various configurations of chairs, but I could feel, from that first moment of recognizing Jim, that something was happening to me—that a match had been struck somewhere way down in the depths.

Anyway, Jim's story:

He'd been the director of the Wright Museum for almost ten years, from the early 2000s until a few months before Hannah and I moved in. The first seven or eight years of his tenure had been completely unremarkable, or no more remarkable than being the director of any other tiny failing history museum would have been: budget cuts, fundraising schemes, meetings with the local school board. He lived at the museum alone ("... my wife had the good sense to divorce me before I started on any of this"). He cooked for himself using herbs from the garden plot. He bickered with Donna and planned weekend events and talked what few visitors the museum had into a state of baffled submission. At night he read seven-hundred-page library books about the tribal history of the Hudson Valley.

Then, at some point in his seventh or eighth year at the house, something strange had happened. "You've got to understand, this was a winter when I was having a lot of health problems. Inner-ear stuff, lung stuff, stomach stuff. So I was unusually susceptible." He was lying in bed one night, keeping himself awake with his coughing, when he suddenly realized that someone was standing in his room watching him. "The room—well, you know how dark the room is. And to get in there, you would have to ... But I could feel the person, exactly the same as I can feel you. So I was trying to decide what to do, should I sit up or shout something or should I just lie there pretending to be asleep, when it happened. The only way I can describe it is, the person, whatever it was, it leapt on me—but instead of attacking me, instead of doing anything like that, it just ... sunk into me. So now I was just lying there in the dark again." But the thoughts he found himself thinking now, the memories he found himself having—they weren't his, they belonged to someone else. Something, someone, was inside him now. And it wasn't until four or five in the morning ("That night was just endless, endless") that he realized who that someone was: Edmund Wright.

Jim didn't tell anyone what had happened to him. "To be honest, I was afraid I was losing my fucking mind." He had, of course, known that there was some loopy ghost-related stuff in Edmund Wright's past, and he'd indulged the Wrighters about it, but he'd never taken it seriously himself. He'd always assumed, the way almost everyone assumed, that this was Conan-Doyle-with-his-fairies stuff—a great mind, under the influence of grief and maybe some nineteenth-century drugs, coming unglued. But now, after the episode in his bed, Jim became convinced that there was more to it than that—that Wright had not only studied spirits but become one. "And I got obsessed. Writing out accounts of what had happened to me, seeing if I could get it to happen again. Reading everything I could get my hands on.

Writing letters to people who I thought might have some old papers in their attics about this stuff."

But he'd only been at it for a couple of weeks when he ran into a roadblock. As soon as Donna found out what kind of research he was doing ("I went to the bathroom and I left a goddamn browser window open"), she started going after him. "This woman, you've got to understand, she is not well. She is unhealthily fixated on . . . she's obsessed with the fact that Edmund Wright was her great-great-whatever-he-was, and if she finds out that anyone's even having a *thought* that she thinks might hurt Wright's reputation, she launches a federal investigation." Butch tried to defend him ("Butch actually knows much more about this stuff than he lets on. He knew the Kemps growing up. Knew them personally"), but even together Butch and Jim were no match for Donna. She convinced the board that Jim wasn't well and that they needed to decrease his responsibilities. She started messing with the heat in the museum. She told Lydia Gibbens ("that absolute joke of a human being"), who was the authority on all things Wright, to send Jim a letter explaining how absurd his line of inquiry was.

But in the meantime—and by this point in the telling Jim was gnawing at his nails so vigorously that one of them had started to bleed—he was continuing to make discoveries about the spirit world. Donna could reduce his responsibilities, she could ruin his reputation, but she couldn't control what he did at night when he was alone in the museum. Wright's spirit had entered him a few more times in the weeks since it had first happened—he could feel, when he was getting ready for bed, whether the conditions were right for it—and he'd started to develop more control of the experience. He could now remember, for instance, on the mornings after his inhabitations, exactly what he'd experienced. It had mostly been a single scene, Jim said: Edmund Wright, alone at the desk in his study, drinking something bitter from a small blue bottle and then slowly losing consciousness. This, when Wright was inhabiting him, was what he would experience over and over.

And he discovered other things, too—for instance that he could write down the story of Wright's death while he experienced it; and that Wright was just one of the spirits in the house. He felt himself inhabited one night by a woman he was fairly sure was Jan Kemp. Another time he thought it was a cat who'd died years before in the basement. Every living being who'd ever been killed in the house was there, he said. "This"—he reached over and flicked my pocket—"is what your girlfriend was up to with her list."

But that wasn't all. Spirits, he said, do more than just make you relive their deaths; that's just what they do while they're getting used to you as a vehicle. Once they're comfortable inside you, they start playing your mind like an instrument. They show you visions. Horrible ones, even things from your own life. During those nights of being inhabited, he reexperienced a childhood memory of plucking the legs off a spider. He saw himself as an old man, choking on his own tongue. For spirits, he realized, the living were like books on a shelf: readable from the first page to the last.

By this point, Jim said, he was "figuring it's either the Nobel Prize or a straitjacket for me. Because these inhabitations, they were lasting longer and longer. I was piecing together whole theories, which people become spirits and where they are, and I'm getting frantic, worrying that someone else discovered this stuff and is going to beat me to it. And then I realize—I was up there in the storage room going through some papers one night—I realized that someone did beat me to it, all of it, by about a century and a half. Edmund Wright."

Because Jim had discovered that winter that there were large and suspicious gaps in Edmund Wright's official papers. "You ask Lydia Gibbens, you ask Donna, you look in the published works, you'd think spirits were just one of Wright's little side interests, like the thing with cross-fertilizing carrots. It's bullshit. The truth is he spent years on this. He wrote a letter to William James calling this the work of his life." Sometimes in the original copies of Wright's journals, Jim explained, there would be a reference to months Wright had spent trying to solve some particular spirit-related problem, but if you went back and tried to find those months of notes, they would just be gone. Same deal with the letters. Certain pages didn't even look like they were in Wright's handwriting.

"Somebody—I think it's got to be his wife—went through and tossed almost every word he ever wrote about ghosts, about spirit writing, all of it, right in the fireplace. The stuff that I found is just the tip of the tip of the iceberg. And whoever it was left just enough so we'd think we had the whole picture. Completely unconscionable. Worst crime against intellectual history since the burning of the Library of Alexandria."

And Jim thought he knew why Wright's wife would have wanted to hide what Wright had been working on. Wright hadn't died of accidental poisoning, the way the Lydia Gibbenses of the world would have you believe. He'd died because the spirits had killed him—that is, they'd shown him something so awful that Wright hadn't been able to bear it and had killed himself. This is what spirits do; this is what they're after with the visions they show you. They *want* you dead, so they can get reincarnated in your place. That's how they get free. They probably would have killed Jim, too, if his health hadn't fallen apart.

"I wasn't sleeping, I wasn't eating, I was hardly ever leaving the museum." He'd developed holes in the lining of his stomach, he said, plus his hip was crumbling, and the problem with his ears had changed so that now, in addition to being dizzy all the time, he heard the sound of rushing water whenever he stood up. "Except I couldn't take time out to go to the doctor, because a doctor would tell me to take a break from the museum." He was right on the cusp of something, he felt. Just days away from discovering the vision that had killed Wright and Jan Kemp. He had more or less given up on running the museum to pursue this question—by this point spirits were coming into him every night—when he got so sick that he passed out on the way to the bathroom and cracked his skull on the toilet tank. When Donna found him in the morning she thought he was dead—his eyes were half open, his tongue was hanging out, blood was all over the tiles.

But he wasn't dead, and the doctors in Poughkeepsie, once they'd cleaned him up and tested him for everything they could think of, told him there wasn't anything physically wrong with him other than high blood pressure and a sinus infection. He was admitted to Sommers on a Sunday afternoon, officially terminated by the Wright House on Monday morning. No matter what he said, the doctors wouldn't let him have his papers from the museum. He started taking half a milligram of Haldol three times daily, plus eight milligrams of Rozerem for sleep. He'd been here babbling to his fellow patients, scribbling notes for his memoirs with a felt-tipped pen, ever since.

I can't explain how hearing all this affected me, exactly—can't reconstruct the moment when I went from listening to him as a skeptic to listening to him as a potential disciple—except to say that I was, by the time he finished, shivering to the base of my spine, and not from caffeine poisoning. Hannah's list was in my sweaty hands.

monday - woman on bridge
tuesday - bird on porch
thursday - boy in wheel
saturday - cat in basement

I had, I felt, arrived at the point where I needed to make a choice. I could believe that what I'd heard was just a Russian nesting doll of insanity: that Jim lived inside Wright's craziness, and that Hannah, thanks to bad luck and some organic predisposition, had come to live inside Jim's. Or I could believe—at the risk of becoming the innermost doll myself—that Jim, and so Hannah, had glimpsed something real, and that all the work I'd done in the hospital was just a complicated means of rejecting the stray bits of oddity that had been begging me to assemble them since Hannah's death.

"Your girlfriend," Jim said. "It sounds like she was following right in my footsteps. Those papers you've got, they would have been the least of it. You said she was always writing in a notebook, right? That's the mother lode. She probably would have tried to hide it. She wouldn't have wanted Donna to find it, maybe not even you. That's what you've got to find."

I sat silent for a few seconds. "What does it mean when you say spirits want to get free? Free from what?"

"From what? From not having a body, from reliving their deaths over and over. It's got to be agony."

I nodded numbly. So this was how grief-sick widowers ended up signing over their life savings to psychics on the Lower East Side. This was how otherwise intelligent people came to fill their houses with quartz crystals and sage bundles. If I could, by taking Hannah too seriously now, make up for having failed to take her seriously enough in the fall, then I was ready to toss away my sanity like a crumpled dollar bill.

I cleared my throat and leaned so close to Jim that our knees were touching. "Do you know if anyone's ever broken out of here?" I said.

[From Lydia Gibbens, *Edmund Wright: A Life*, published by the Dutchess County Historical Society, Notable Figures Series]

... That Wright was, by the middle of that winter, in a state of great despondency is indisputable. Producing fewer and fewer pages, beset as ever by money troubles, he had turned once again for relief to that reliable friend, laudanum. It is the bitterest of ironies that Wright, whose career had been built on scrupulous experimental practices, would be undone by something so trivial as a routine mismeasurement ...

Summer 2069—New Jersey—Age 88

*You are sitting in the sun by the window where they've left your
chair you start to reach for your glass of wine but your hand is
shaking lately you've been dropping things pens glasses silverware your sister has been talking without taking a breath now
she asks do you remember Denise you tell her yes of course you
smile that seems to satisfy her you reach again for the glass but
your fingers won't open they seem not to belong to you your sister
raises her eyebrows says you really do seem so much better she
takes a handful of almonds drops them in her mouth you smile
again say what you'd really like is to be out of this chair and you
don't mention the night last week when you fell from the bed the
floor rushing up to meet you the dark crawl to the phone the rest
on the carpet and how you had never until that second unable
to move your arms or call for help or lift your head you had never
understood before just what it meant to be alone . . .*

[Incident Report, Department of Security,
Northern Dutchess Hospital]

Name (Print):
Peter H. Israel

Pass #:
123102

Security Incident #:
E – 32 – 1250 – 15

Time of Report:
17:25

Supervisor Notified:
YES

Time Notified:
17:35

Incident Report Details:
I was notified by hospital staff over the radio to check the
emergency exit door in the lounge because a maintenance
worker had reported seeing it open. Upon checking the
door it was open. After consulting Officer Clery I declared
a E-2202 and followed protocol, contacting Dr. Gutman

via radio (unavailable). Officer Clery asked me to assist him + staff in conducting headcount. 25/26 Sommers patients were accounted for. Missing patient concluded to be NICHOLAS BERON, Room 314, Age 30, Admit Date 12/14. Conducted brief search of ward + stairwells + hospital perimeter, after which Officer Clery instructed me to notify Dutchess County PD, send Beron's patient ID photo + info. I did so (16:55–17:00). I then assisted Officer Clery + staff conducting E-2202 patient interviews 17:00–18:15 (notes attached).

Condition Resolved:
No

Further Comments:
In my opinion JAMES MCCLARAN (Room 302) and DIEGO ORTIZ (Room 314) should receive extra questioning.

PART THREE

. . .

1

Breaking out of Northern Dutchess Hospital turns out to require approximately the same level of ingenuity it takes to be admitted to it. For almost a week Jim and I, with Diego as our third wheel, played *Escape from Alcatraz*—whispering at the bathroom sinks, watching the security guards on their afternoon rounds, speaking in code ("shoe" meant "ID badge"; "Bobby" was "Sean," the guard whose card we'd decided it would be the easiest to steal). The actual escape took all of fifteen minutes, and, except for the presence of one startled nurse's aide vaping at the bottom of a stairwell, went off without a hitch. Signs that say "Emergency Exit Alarm WILL Sound" very rarely mean what they say. Bystanders who see that something is off tend, especially in a place as brimming with staff as a hospital, to assume that someone else will be the one to deal with it.

It was five o'clock when I emerged panting into the parking lot/loading dock behind Building Three; it was already dark out, raining halfheartedly. All I had with me were my toothbrush and a few pairs of underwear and socks, all wrapped hobo-style in an old sweatshirt of Hannah's. There was no siren blaring, no policeman shouting into his bullhorn from a guard tower. Just the rain on the pavement and a couple of distant cars honking. On one side of the parking lot was a stand of bare trees; on the other was a windowless brick building that looked like it might house an incinerator. The air, just the quantity of it that was available to me as I set off along one of the empty exit roads, felt like a massive black lake.

I should say here that my faith—my conviction that Hannah, and so Jim, and so Wright, were nondelusional—had begun to waver in the days before I left the hospital, so I had, in order to maintain what remained of my self-respect, started building myself an internal cover story. It wasn't necessarily, I'd begun to tell myself, that I believed in the truth of whatever Hannah thought she had discovered; it was just that I wouldn't understand how she'd died unless I understood exactly what *she* thought she'd discovered. So I wasn't, by returning to Wright, proving that I'd had a mental breakdown; I was conducting a psychological investigation of a crime scene. In her notebook I'd find the story that really would be good enough.

My first civilian stop was at a Dunkin' Donuts a quarter mile south of the hospital on Route 9—this was in a strip mall featuring a GNC and a vacant, ghost-lettered Price Chopper. Being any sort of fugitive makes even ordinary sentences ("Glazed, please") sound squirrelly. The Bluetooth-wearing man behind the cash register didn't look up at me, though; I don't think he could have identified me in a lineup of two. I inhaled half a dozen donut holes there on the sidewalk, working my lips over the wrinkled wax paper like a giraffe, and then, from what must have been the last working pay phone in Dutchess County, I collect-called my dad.

A minivan pulled past while I stood shivering, waiting for the call to connect, and I did my best, despite the pajama pants and sandals, to look as if I were conducting a piece of ordinary business, maybe calling my wife to see if I should pick up some eggs. I'd put Hannah's sweatshirt on over my T-shirt, which didn't help in my quest to look inconspicuous—it strained over my chest and shoulders and only went down to my belly button—

but the temperature was dropping and the rain had become mixed with something like flecks of Slurpee.

"Hello? Nick?" My dad's voice overlapped with the robot-operator saying that the charges had been accepted. I told my dad, turning my back to the parking lot while I spoke, about having left the hospital, about needing to go take care of something. I didn't use the words *escape* or *Hannah* or, needless to say, *ghosts.*

"What are you doing? You need to be in the hospital. They were helping you. Where are you? Call them up and tell them you made a mistake."

"I'm not going back. I'm just calling because the police are going to call and I don't want you to freak out. Don't tell them you talked to me."

"Jesus, Nick—"

"I'm asking you. Just say you have no idea. And I need you to call Mom and tell her the same thing, okay? Can you do that? Just tell her that I'm fine."

I could see him taking off his glasses, massaging his forehead with his fingertips. "Well, tell me where you are, at least. I can call someone to pick you up. They can bring you wherever you need to go."

"I'm fine. Just remember to call Mom. Okay?"

He was silent for a second—I wondered if he was calling the hospital on the other line—and when he spoke again he sounded a hundred years old. "How did this happen?"

"I just walked out. It's not like there's a moat."

"But how did it come to this? You were getting help ... and now you're running away from the hospital, the police—"

"I don't know what to say," I told him. "My life hasn't been going exactly how I want it to. I need to hang up."

It only took forty-five minutes for me to find my way from

the strip mall to the train tracks. The commuter rails that criss-cross the Hudson Valley are a godsend to anyone whose circumstances require them to navigate long distances on foot without the aid of a map. My plan—hatched at the public computer in the hospital lounge, with the browser in Incognito mode—was to walk fifteen miles north along the tracks to the Wassaic station, and then to let half-familiarity and road signs steer me to Hibernia. The tracks, where I joined them, were rusty and spottily lit, set along the spine of a long mound of gravel. I walked ten or so feet from the tracks, in a little gully by the edge of the woods, stopping every few minutes to pull gravel or a twig bit out of my sandals.

By the time I'd been walking for an hour or so—two trains had clattered past, each one consisting of literally countless massive cars—the sleet had picked up to the point that Hannah's sweatshirt was plastered to my shoulders and the socks and underwear in my hands were as soaked as if I'd just pulled them out of the washing machine. There were ice chips in my pants and in the neck of my sweatshirt. The occasional platforms I passed were like small towns along an endless highway; each one held a cluster of umbrella-wielding commuters who seemed to be not just in better circumstances than mine but in a better universe. I felt like a filthy Russian soldier marching to Siberia; I felt like a dog who's broken hugely, catastrophically free.

I had started, by the time I passed the Pawling station, carrying on a scattered, nonlinear conversation, half with myself, half with Hannah. My lips were moving, but the sounds coming out were less than words. *What happened?* I mumbled. *Where did you go? Why didn't you teach me how to find you there?*

It was dark enough now, and it had been long enough since a train had gone by, that I had started to suspect, incoherently, that I had somehow missed a fork and wandered off along some defunct set of tracks. My mind had entered that unreliable, sleep-adjacent state in which it seemed possible I might have hallucinated the entire walk. I was a few minutes past Dover Plains—this was the most crowded platform I'd seen yet—when this unreliability cleared away, or deepened, to produce the sensation that someone was following me. I could hear footsteps crunching gingerly along behind me, and when I stopped to listen to them, they would stop, replaced by the sound of someone breathing shallowly. Nothing was visible behind me except an ominous murk. I imagined a state trooper, newish on the job, creeping along with one hand on his weapon. I imagined a mountain lion with razor teeth and worn-velvet paws. Nothing connects you to your prey-animal past like a bout of outdoor paranoia; I could practically feel my nostrils twitching.

When the sense of huntedness became intolerable I ran a few feet from the tracks and walked the next mile or two through dark brambles farther from the gravel and the light. Thorn bushes looped along the ground like barbed wire. Tree branches kept appearing at perfect face-whapping height. I was convinced, with every squelching step I took, that at any moment a policeman's shouting or an animal's jaws were going to swallow me up, and I wasn't at all sure that either of these would be a worse fate than just continuing to feel the way I felt. *Keep walking, keep walking, keep walking.* A train roared past, startling me and setting off a serrated scrape of pain along the back of my skull. I was far enough into the woods now, and it was dark enough, that I could only tell if the liquid on my cheek was water or blood by tasting it. The part of me, already small, that had any faith whatsoever in the wisdom of what I was doing was shrinking toward nonexistence.

When I finally saw the Wassaic platform—a yellow-lit oasis half-glimpsed through dark brambles—I had just been trying to decide whether it would make more sense for me to lie down here or to go off in search of a phone to call the hospital. Long walks aren't over until you've spent a few minutes convinced that you may, instead of finishing, just have to die.

I staggered soaking out of the woods and across the tracks, having glanced both ways to make sure I was going to be neither killed nor ambushed, then I climbed, like Sasquatch hauling himself out of a swimming pool, up onto the empty and unlit end of the platform. A woman in a silver raincoat at the far end of the platform either saw me or just happened to tilt her head in my direction. The PA announcement implored us all to keep an eye on our belongings. I hurried down the stairs into the parking lot and out onto the sidewalk next to Deep Hollow Road. *If they were going to catch you they would have already caught you. Manhunts are for terrorists and ax murderers. They probably haven't even noticed that you're gone.* Deep Hollow led to 22 led to 44 led to 82 led, after what must have been a couple of hours, to landmarks I actually recognized. Williams Lumber was closed and its Pepsi machine was unplugged; the billboard for Hudson Valley Toyota looked like someone had torn it halfway down and then thought better of it. *Every traumatic death is a mystery. How close am I to solving yours? What did you see what did you think what did you do what did you write and if I find it out can I be absolved can I sleep through the night can I see a woman your age without imagining it might be you can you show me how to bear your death my life?*

I walked past the firehouse, the antique store, the town hall, the laundromat. The houses and houses and houses. Landscapes change so slowly when you're on foot. Even this last, non-train-track, non-highway stretch of my walk couldn't have taken less than two hours; my feet had long since stopped registering distinct sensations—I felt like I was walking on stumps of frozen steak. I kept putting my filthy fingers in my mouth, to thaw them out. I could feel that something bad was starting to happen around the edges of my ears. A little past Peck's a white pickup truck stopped next to me—a man in a backward baseball cap leaned out and asked if I was okay—and I don't know what my look conveyed, but he sped off without my having to say a word.

I finally turned onto Culver at what must have been close to midnight. There aren't streetlights in Hibernia, once you get past the town, so all I could see of things were pale chalk outlines: road here, fields there, woods as squares of black. *If I die of pneumonia will your parents come to my funeral? Will the firehouse change its sign in my memory?* The sleet was making a sound like a thousand tiny drum rolls. The house with the corn crib had its porch lights on. My teeth were chattering, and I'd discovered that it warmed me up—or maybe just distracted me—if I sung a wavering, continuous *v-v-v* whenever I wasn't talking to myself. So I was droning, and digging my fingernails into my palms, thinking pain might help too, when the road took a curve that I knew in the depths of my empty stomach. There was the fallen barn. There were the birch trees. And there, at the top of its hill, faint as a stone through dark water, was the Wright House.

.   .   .

The plan I'd worked out, if you can call it a plan, had two parts: I needed to find Hannah's notebook, and I needed to teach myself the ghost-courting technique that Hannah and Jim and Wright had learned. But before I could start on either one, I had some immediate animal needs to take care of: warmth, hygiene, nourishment.

The museum, from the outside, looked so completely dark, so uninhabited, that it could just as well have been an unusually large shed. The front door was locked, and the key that Hannah and I had taken to hiding on top of the middle porch-pillar wasn't there. The windows were locked too, and, in the back of the house, so was the door into the caretaker's apartment. My only consideration, then, was which window to break, and what to do if/when the alarm went off.

I chose a particularly solid piece of firewood from the pile by the side of the house—a piece of wood that would, thanks to having been left out in the rain, have led to the most sputtering and miserable fire—and I walked quietly around to the back door. No neighbors' windows were close enough for them to see me. No cars were on the road. So this, I thought, is how crimes beget crimes. With one satisfying motion I battering-rammed the log end first through the windowpane closest to the doorknob, a feeling like bashing a pumpkin with a baseball bat. Then I reached through the window, careful not to scrape my arm, and I let myself in. The alarm wasn't sounding as I re-locked the door behind me, and it still wasn't sounding as I peeled off my wet clothes and tossed the soaking fabric heap into the mudroom sink. Just to be safe I went over to the wall panel and punched in Hannah's all-purpose four-digit code, 2734. There wasn't so much as a flicker of acknowledging light.

It took me, despite the alarm, and despite the failure of every light switch I tried, a surprising number of minutes to realize that the house's electricity had been turned off. And it took me longer than it should have after that to realize that this meant that the house wasn't going to have heat, either. It was cold enough inside that my newly exposed skin—I was wearing just my boxers and T-shirt—felt like rotisserie chicken fresh from the refrigerator.

I made my way, via baby steps and wall patting—and with just one barking of my shin against a low stool—to the closet near Hannah's office, where I thought I remembered seeing the candles and candlesticks we'd used in the Spooky Halloween Festival. I felt blindly around the shelves, between cardboard boxes and unidentified small appliances, until my fingers encountered a box of cool wax cylinders, and next to them a row of metal candlesticks. Below the candlesticks, on a newspaper-and-mouse-poop stretch of shelf, I felt the bent cardboard contours of an almost-empty box of matches. Let there be a creepy sort of light.

Holding my candle by the candlestick's too-small finger loop, I reacquainted myself with the main part of the house. The shadows cast by the candle flame seemed to vibrate. The furniture, most of it, had been covered in what looked like tattered bedsheets.

In the back corner of the parlor, below the row of coat pegs, I found the costume trunk, still rusty latched, still brimming. Fleabag coats and cotton shirts and hoop dresses and bonnets. I set my candle on a table and pulled together an outfit that would have embarrassed a nineteenth-century flasher, and then staggered my way, itching and encumbered, into the caretaker's apartment.

My hunger, like a well-behaved child, had waited until it had a reasonable hope of satisfaction to notify me of the urgency of its situation. The only food left in the cabinets, though—the same cabinets that Hannah and I had once filled with almond butter and dry spaghetti and chocolate-cherry granola bars— was an ancient box of pancake mix and a slippery canister of olive oil. It required less time than you might think to resign myself to my options. I poured myself the most revolting sort of mouth-pancake—three parts dry pancake mix, one part rancid olive oil—and I swallowed the paste down greedily. I repeated this process, coughing and gagging, until I'd emptied both box and canister.

My plan had been to sleep on our old bare mattress in the caretaker's apartment, but the room seemed somehow to be even colder than the rest of the house—I now remembered Hannah saying something about us needing to buy a space heater. So I wandered back out into the museum, a divining rod in search of warmth. Not the kitchen exhibit, not the entryway, not the living room. I creaked and shuffled my way up the stairs to the second floor, carrying my candle like a brimming bowl of soup. The top stair creaked and I nearly brained myself when I tripped on the landing. Not the storage room, not the children's bedroom, not the exhibit room in which the cases stood empty and the wall signs still promised a look at Wright's Famous Encyclopedias.

I'm not sure if it was my imagination or the warmth that over- comes a person at a certain point in his descent into delirium, but in Edmund and Sarah's bedroom, finally, I thought I felt a type of cold that had a slightly less painful edge to it. I touched the bed, remembered the Styrofoam peanuts, and yanked off the period quilt, bringing with it a cloud of dust that I could taste.

For a second I just stood there, my heart racing, the quilt heaped at my feet, and took in my situation. This is where you are. This is the moment to which your particular life has delivered you.

I curled up on the little hooked rug at the foot of the Wrights' bed, using the quilt as mattress, blanket, and, thanks to some creative folding, pillow. I certainly wasn't warm, but I was covered, which is the next best thing. I had set the candle on the floor next to my head, near enough that I could feel, or imagine that I was feeling, some of its heat. I didn't want to blow it out yet, because I'd forgotten to bring the matches upstairs and I wasn't ready to consign myself to a night of total darkness, so I just watched the flame wobble and limbo for a while. But I bolted awake after some number of minutes and realized that the only thing worse than being woken up by the police would be to be woken up by an inferno. So I blew the candle out, watched the wick tip fade, smelled birthday party. Dear God it was so dark. *What did you do what am I doing what have I done.* The only sound was the rain on the roof and a whispering I very much hoped was just blood rushing in my ears.

And this—despite my having resolved not to start in on my ghost work until the morning—was when the first mental channel slippage happened. The only way I can describe it is to say that at some point as I lay there, I started flickering into lives that weren't mine. I was touching the iron railing of a bridge ... and then I was back on the floor in the Wrights' bedroom. I was leaning forward over a messy desk ... and then I was myself again, panting under my quilt.

I don't know how long I lay there, passing in and out of ordinary consciousness, but it was long enough for me to formulate a prayer: *If this is anything like what Jim experienced, then I don't think I'm ready for it. I may just have to die.* At one point I sat upright, certain I'd heard a knocking on the wall by the closet. At another point I spent a good five minutes deliberating about whether to get up and pee. I felt increasingly aware, with each second that passed, of how little padding there was between my hip bones and the floor. I kept getting whiffs of mold or mildew or dead animal. The last coherent thought I remember having, before I finally sunk into an unrefreshing sleep, was: Am I, this trembling, hallucinating ball of sinew, really any stranger of a creature, any more improbable of an object, than a ghost?

[from Edmund Wright, *The Encyclopedia of Ordinary Human Sensation*, volume II: *Pleasures*, edited by Lydia Gibbens]

. . .

- The sudden stoppage of a meddlesome sound, viz. the newsboy's shouts or a team of horses' hooves.

- The near-certain knowledge, derived from certain atmospheric and behavioral clues, that one's partner intends to fulfill the act of coitus.

- The sensation in one's extremities when initially settling into bed, after a day that has been trying, whether physically or intellectually or emotionally or any combination thereof.

- The singing of a pure and muscular note, quite precisely inhabiting the pitch one intended.

- The minority of dreams, viz. dreams of hearing a most hilarious joke (which hilarity nearly invariably fails to translate into one's waking senses); dreams in which one composes music, or speaks an unknown language, or in any other way demonstrates a heretofore unsuspected creative faculty; dreams of sexual fulfillment *with a proper and intended partner;* dreams of transformation, either of one's own body or of external objects, into shapes that are both pleasing and contain the element of inevitability.

·   The realization that one has, in the course of one's researches, arrived at the moment when one's fundamental question shall be answered imminently.

. . .

2

One of Hannah's more durable and justified complaints about me, when we were together, was that I didn't know how to look for things. I would, standing in front of a refrigerator featuring multiple bottles of mustard, insist that we were out. I would pillage the apartment in search of a pair of glasses that were resting on the edge of the bathroom sink.

Alone in the museum that next morning, I was determined to do better. I didn't quite have Jim's faith that Hannah had hidden her notebook in the house—it seemed just as likely to be at the bottom of Donna's box, or at the bottom of the river—but my operating principle, at that point, was to do anything that had even the slightest chance of bringing me closer to her.

So I started out in the main parts of the house, dividing each room into quadrants like an archaeologist. This was, incidentally, a search conducted entirely with the curtains drawn, and with a good quarter of my attention absorbed in listening for tires on the driveway or footsteps on the porch. I was still wearing the loose white shirt and wool coat from the costume trunk. I looked under the carpets, inside drawers, underneath dressers. I lifted cushions from armchairs and took books off of shelves. I was, by the time I'd been at it for an hour or so, in that same state of desperation and mounting despair as if I'd been looking for my passport in the minutes before needing to leave for a trip. There was nothing but printer cartridges and dry pens in Hannah's old office, nothing but broken-down shelving in the closet across from the stairs. In the storage room upstairs, underneath a stack of blank teacher evaluation forms, I found a torn piece of Wright House notepaper with Hannah's handwriting on it— my blood briefly froze—but it was just an 845 phone number and the beginning of a shopping list. What had I been thinking? The museum was almost as cold now as it had been at night; I could feel my hopelessness—my sense of being fundamentally doomed and delusional—threatening to swallow me up. Fearing that you've lost your mind turns out to be no more romantic, and no easier to bear, than fearing that you have bowel cancer.

I spent most of that afternoon on the couch downstairs in the parlor, trying to convince myself that my ghost work might go better than my notebook hunting. Make yourself receptive, had been Jim's instruction. Relax your muscles and turn your mind into an empty room. So I sat there watching the light change on the floorboards, pleading with Hannah to help me, feeling my face break into tears and then reassemble itself. How were you supposed to relax when every breeze sounded like a knock at the door and every inch of your body ached? How were you supposed to empty your mind when you couldn't stop looking at the crack between the curtains? *Hannah,* I muttered, *if what I'm doing has the slightest chance of succeeding, if I'm not just falling apart, please show me how, please show me something.* But no one appeared and nothing happened. I only realized how long I'd been sitting there—and how easily I could have stayed sitting there forever—when I saw that the room was now dark enough that I was going to need another candle soon. Which meant that it had been more than twenty-four hours since I'd eaten a real meal.

I considered, briefly, breaking into a neighbor's house— maybe the family down Culver with the softball tee—and emptying out their fridge. Or maybe walking back into town, seeing what I could steal from the bins by the farm stand. The plan I eventually settled on, though—and I can't vouch for my decision-making in this period—was to see if I could find anything edible in the museum's garden. I'd seen Hannah pull up some knobby little carrots once, and I remembered watching her plant some knuckle-sized potato pieces at some point that fall. Even in the winter, didn't there have to be at least something under there? My mouth actually watered at the thought of half-frozen vegetable stubs. My knowledge of harvest cycles was as spotty as my knowledge of the spirit world.

So I scurried out to the garden plot, prepared to flee back inside if I spotted anyone. This was my first venture into open air since coming back to the museum. The sky was silver mixed with gray, and the wind bit directly into the square inch of chest where my shirt was missing a button. The ground was hard but not, I found when I leaned over, completely frozen. Here was the deer fence around the garden that Butch and I had spent a sunny afternoon building; here were the beams that Hannah and I had dragged off a pickup truck for the raised beds.

With a spade from the shed I started scraping away at the first plot. I had my shirt sleeve pulled down over my hand instead of a glove. Eventually I uncovered some dead and frozen sage leaves, but one nibble revealed that they were too miserable even for me. The second plot had been overtaken entirely by a woody reddish vine that kept snagging on my pants. In the third plot—under a mound still marked with weathered popsicle sticks—I found my first hope of sustenance: a scattering of tiny, filthy potatoes that, collectively, couldn't have weighed a pound; I held the entire harvest (which I quickly realized included a couple of potato-colored rocks) in my cupped hands.

I won't go into the trouble it took me to build a fire in the fireplace, or the process by which I convinced myself that it was now dark enough, and that the fire would be small enough, that no passersby would notice the smoke curling out of the chimney. I'll just say that these potatoes, roasted to the edge of edibility in a historic cast iron pot, were more precious to me than any restaurant meal I'd ever eaten. No wonder our ancestors were so hardy; every calorie was once wrested from the earth like a prisoner of war.

I was going through some old binders in Hannah's office after dinner—newly fortified, and perhaps lulled into a mild state of slackness, by my potatoes—when I heard, from the front of the house, what sounded very much like gravel crunching and an engine turning off. For a few seconds I sat holding my breath, considering blowing out my candle, wondering whether this could be another hallucination. Hours of anxiously awaiting something do not, it turns out, make the arrival of that thing any less alarming. I shrank back in my chair. And here, before I could think what to do next, were human voices. And now here were footsteps on the porch.

I grabbed my candle and, cupping the flame, raced down the stairs into the basement. When Hannah and I had lived in the museum, I had avoided the basement at all costs; it was my every atavistic terror in the form of a room. The staircase consisted of unmoored two-by-fours. The floor was cold dirt. The walls were stone, meaning made from actual, irregular stones. The ceiling, fiberglass and rusty pipes, was low enough that you had to hunch. And it was now, since even the bulb with the chain didn't work, as dark as the inside of a coffin.

I went and crouched by the boiler—which was as cold as something dead—and focused on making my breathing quiet. My candle made a ball of light that illuminated nothing but my shaking hands. The whole room seemed to swim with evil. And I could hear, as if I were below the floorboards at a theater, someone knocking at the front door, then muffled voices, then more knocking. And after a minute, with no warning (and this is when my heartbeat became loud enough that I worried it might be audible through the floor), I heard footsteps inside the house.

I'd forgotten the precise terror of being It in hide-and-seek. The voices—there were two male voices, one of them vaguely familiar—sounded much less distinct than the footsteps. I could hear every heel strike and board creak as whoever it was walked from the front hall into the caretaker's apartment and then back into the living room. Their conversation was strangely sparse—a calm, professional sort of talk. After a couple of minutes I heard the familiar voice say, "Did you get this?" and I listened as one of them shifted something heavy, cursing myself for not having cleaned up my potato dinner.

This went on, this Foley performance of footsteps and pauses and half-audible conversation, for what felt like an hour but really couldn't have been more than twenty minutes. At some point one or both of them went up to the second floor and the sounds got more distant for a while. My fingers were covered in dribbles of white wax. The seat of my pants was either wet or just very cold. When the footsteps came back down to the first floor I heard the familiar voice make a joke—it sounded like "Corn money?"—and then the other one answer with a short, unamused laugh. The footsteps were directly overhead now, so close that I worried they might hear my candle sputtering. They weren't saying anything. A walkie-talkie, or something, crackled. And then, just at the moment when I was sure they were going to burst into the basement—I'd decided I would fling myself to the ground and cover my head with my coat—I heard someone opening the front door of the house. There was a crescendo of footsteps, a few indiscernible words, and then the front door closing with a forcible bang. Had that really happened? All I could hear now was my breathing. They were gone, just as if they'd never been there at all. This was another hide-and-seek feeling that I'd forgotten.

I stayed there twitching in the dark for a few minutes, in case they were just circling the house, and by the time I finally decided I was safe, enough time had passed, and I had been in a sufficiently uncomfortable position, that getting to my feet was going to require a series of slow-motion maneuvers. I set my candle on the dirt by the boiler, turned onto my hands and knees, and discovered that my feet were the kind of asleep that makes any movement impossible. So I stayed still for a minute, pounding my throbbing feet against the ground, massaging my calves, and when I looked up, I spotted something in the wavering circle of candlelight. It was tucked between the boiler and the wall a few inches off the ground. My first thought was a user's manual: *Boilers for Dummies*, dropped by some long-ago handyman. I extended an arm, in a geriatric yoga pose—the pages, I found as I pried them out from the gap where they'd been crammed, were crushed in at one corner, stained with something damp. It was a notebook with a black-and-white speckled cover.

[Edmund Wright's journal]

Dec. 8

. . .

How peculiar that the plainest human life—with its innumerable pleasures & pains; its ceaseless vulnerability; the endless sense of having almost but not quite attained some crucial, unnameable thing; its inevitable end . . . How very odd that this most common of conditions can, from a certain angle of perception, seem the material for a tale of such surpassing cruelty that not even the most Gothic of authors would . . .

. . .

3

I deliberated for a ridiculously long time about where to read Hannah's notebook: when someone can't summon the courage to do something, acts of preparation take on special significance. It was pitch-black out by the time I came up from the basement, and for a long time I just paced around the house with my candle and the notebook, like a lunatic in a Poe story. I settled on Hannah's storage room upstairs, finally. A part of me, I realized, had the feeling that I was about to betray her, and to go into this room—the room that I associated so strongly with everything that had happened to her—felt like an act of pre-absolution. I would baptize myself in her aura.

So I settled in with her notebook in the spot where she used to sit, on the little red cushion on the floor by the window. All around me were binders and boxes and stray bits of curiosity-shop garbage—a folded flag; a copper eagle; a waist-high jumble of empty picture frames. I put my candle on an empty stretch of windowsill. I held a pencil from her desk downstairs, in case I needed to make notes. The room, in the candlelight, was the color of the inside of a tent, with soft-edged shadows. It gets hard, at a certain point, to tell what sounds are coming from inside your head; I heard buzzing and shaking and a high wavering whine.

In order to see the page I had to hold the notebook up close to the candle with my left hand, so my posture as I read had a strange supplicating quality to it, like a priest with a crucifix. The first pages, sparsely written, seemed to be just ordinary work stuff:

- *Call JM re 10/22 event (24 people; chairs?)*
- *Find out when we did cooking exhibition 2009 & 2010*
- *Conf call Tues at 4:30, dial-in #4589785 (tell D)*
- *Get toothpicks, cups, dirt (McKeough's?)*

Hannah, I thought, *sweet, sane, conscientious Hannah. Could this really have been you? Have I really been chasing after something this un-mysterious?* Maybe Dr. Mital's good-enough story—that Hannah had succumbed to a mental illness no more otherworldly than a stroke, and that the only complications were in my imagination—really had been true.

But a few pages in, after a blank page and then a few that had been torn out (these, it occurred to me, might be the lists I'd been carrying in my pocket), things started to get weird.

You are sitting on a low wall beside your sister in a park your toes reach the ground you're wearing a white shirt puffed sleeves short purple shorts your shoes are cheetah-patterned a gnat is struggling to enter your nose your sister says I've never seen mom that pissed you make a noise you don't know whether it means you don't believe her or you don't care

That was all that was written on one page. The handwriting was still Hannah's, but different somehow, more fluid. I made a meaningless line in the margin. My heart had started to pound. I turned a couple of pages ahead.

You are in the backseat green car a blond boy is driving pressing stereo buttons large square fingers the girl next to you is smoking out the window you see the moon low and red over the CVS you feel suddenly like crying but instead you cough . . .

And a few pages after that:

You are lying sideways on a twin bed with rumpled sheets the room is dark there's another girl on the bed across the room who is doing something with her bare feet against the wall hanging Oberlin: Learning & Labor a boy is on the floor between you resting his head you know he would like to kiss you he has been looking for opportunities all night the lights are off the speakers are balanced on a milk crate . . .

The entries were getting longer and longer—some of them were multiple pages now, but I was, for whatever reason, only capable of reading a few lines at a time; I felt like I was racing through a gauntlet of sharpened spears.

You are standing in spotted shade you are facing your husband he is almost your husband your friends your family are sitting in chairs on logs they are fanning themselves your grandmother tiny and ancient is perched in the first row the rabbi is going on too long . . .

You are walking down a brick path your hand is trailing on a black metal gate you are watching your baby he is squatting in rubber boots white wrinkles of diaper fat pale thighs he is digging for something in the dirt his little nails the sprinkler is turning slowly over dry hostas . . .

You are sitting in a hard chair next to your dad who is in a high beige plastic bed your mom is by the window other buildings rows of windows the nineteenth floor she says to no one this is

*absolutely ridiculous these windows must have been designed
by Rube Goldberg . . .*

If my skin had been attached to sensors, the temperature
readout would now have fallen below freezing. My body, some
animal thing in me, had worked out already what all this was.

*You are standing at a metal sink in a white kitchen scrubbing
a pan that won't come clean the party is still going you hear the
laughter like a lapping tide you hear your husband's voice come
in here you watch the water turn white you scrub until your fingers ache . . .*

*You are propped up in a small bed the sheets are tight around
your legs a nurse leans toward you with a spoon says come
on now you've got to eat you tighten your lips she pries them
open your throat is dry the food tastes like something you can't
remember she says that's it that's right you close your eyes . . .*

My brain had now caught up with my body; the feeling was
like an elevator reaching the ground floor too fast, that sicken-
ing thud. These were Hannah's stories; this was Hannah's life.
That wedding was the wedding we would have had. That baby
was the baby we would have had. I can't explain how clearly this
all came to me, how simple it seemed—it was as if something
were pushing me toward the realization, and maybe something
was. *Your girlfriend was possessed by spirits and night after night, while
you slept downstairs oblivious, she wrote out the story of her life.* Spirits
would show you a vision that would drive you insane, Jim had
said, and here it was: your past and future laid out before you
like a book.

I don't know how many times I read through the notebook,
once I understood—I was fully sobbing now, so the words kept

disappearing into a blur. Here was our first dance, here was our son discovering his feet, here was Hannah plucking her eyebrows in front of a hotel mirror, here was her fiftieth-birthday party on the deck of a boat, here was the morning in line at the airport, here was the nursing home. *Are we going to be okay? Are we going to have a happy life?* I kept wiping my eyes with my sleeve, senselessly repeating Hannah's name. So this was the horror that had overtaken her, this was the vision she hadn't known how to bear. "Do you ever get scared just of being alive?" she'd asked me once, mid-breakdown. I'd asked her what she meant but by then the window had closed, it was too late.

For a while, sitting there in the storage room, I tried to write down my best guesses at places and dates next to each entry, to impose some kind of order on the flood that was swallowing me, but by the third or fourth time through I'd given up and was just making lines, little dashes of protest and heartbreak. My nose was running freely to my lips. My candle had burned down to a puddly stub.

Finally, when I didn't think I could read through it another time, I sat back against the wall, limp, with the notebook open to the last page in my lap. The shadows now covered almost the entire walls. My muscles were relaxed, in the way that someone's muscles are relaxed after a lobotomy. My mind was empty, in the way a town square is empty after an atomic bombing. And so, if I'd been capable of thinking clearly, I wouldn't have been surprised by what happened next. My body started to fill up with something both strange and deeply, cellularly familiar. I felt both terrified and liquidly calm. I was, I realized, some part of me was, not myself: I was Hannah walking across a field at dawn. The rest of me, still on the floor with a pencil in my hand, sat up and began to write.

．　　．　　．

*I walked out of the house across the field I was barefoot the sun
hadn't risen I had made up my mind I was so tired I was afraid
I couldn't find the courage to live my life I crossed the hills this is
the last grass the last sky the last morning I came to the riverbank
the sun was almost up the trees were still wet I dragged the canoe
red and heavy down through the grass pushed it out into the water
upside down I wanted you to be okay I wanted you to think I had
been okay now the air was aerosol the sky was scraps of cloud the
edge of the river was reeds cold mud I walked out barefoot god it
was cold not as cold as the air somehow I kept taking steps the
water to my knees then my thighs I did have second thoughts I did
shiver I could still feel where you'd touched me finally my waist
finally deep enough that to go deeper I'd need to swim cold is just
sensation I raised my arms plunged forward something screamed
no but something else lowered my head under the surface the water
was dark green-brown the river was deeper than I thought faster I
told myself not to fight I was in a new sort of space I would forget
and then remember and then forget and then it was like falling
asleep I could feel my thoughts turn strange I couldn't remember
the last time I'd breathed I felt my mind nestling into something
I couldn't find the surface with every second I knew it would be
harder to break out something in me wanted to break out something
else was so content I let myself sink and sink I swallowed water
freezing mud pain is just sensation my lungs didn't hurt anymore
I was slipping down and down regret is just sensation my body*

wasn't me anymore I was leaving and leaving and then it was just a scarecrow that drifted down got caught on a branch I'm sorry I was already gone already here the pain was gone I didn't know there are worse things than pain didn't know I would be trapped here Nick every day and night I live my death I walk into the water I've waited for you please help me I don't know how but Wright did please help me please help me please

· · ·

By the time I woke up with Hannah's notebook in my lap—I must have fallen asleep, or anyway into some sort of state in which time didn't register—the sun was already going down again. My mouth was so dry that I could feel all the slight sand-paper variations inside. My body was excruciatingly stiff, and not just from having spent the past however many hours sitting up against a wall. I thought, honestly, that I might be dead, and that these might be the sensations I was stuck with for all time. The memory of having been Hannah had already slipped behind a dark curtain, as if I'd been under anesthesia.

I stood up, propelled like a sleepwalker or a risen corpse, and stumbled my way downstairs. I didn't have a candle anymore, so I was navigating mainly by leaning against the wall. I made my way out the front door onto the porch—there was a thin line of paler cloud behind some hills where the sun was setting—and I understood, from the way the wind hit my skin and my head ached, that I was in fact alive, however feebly. I knelt down and drank a few freezing hand-cups of filthy water from the culvert next to the driveway. There was no one else out, but walking out onto the road, turning right at the Stop sign, starting almost at a jog along the gravel shoulder up the hill, I knew I wouldn't have cared even if someone was.

I don't think I could have directed someone else to Butch's house—I'd only been there a couple of times when he worked at Wright. And I don't think I was conscious either of why my legs were carrying me there—this plan must have been hatched while I was asleep, or wherever I'd been. My mind had been stirred like a drink and the ice cube that was now bobbing on the surface was one I'd forgotten about completely: *buried, not burned.* So I walked up Cold Spring and left on Amenia and then back into the little tract of houses on the dirt loop that didn't have a name. A tall gray dog was going insane behind an electric fence. A black horse in a plaid jacket was standing staring from the top of a hill. My ordinary consciousness was slowly coming online and I thought it must have been close to five o'clock now; I was aware, walking across the little yard and up the couple of cement steps to Butch's front door, that I might present an alarming sight.

His wife answered the door—I knew it was his wife despite never having met her. She had a long, hawkish, wary face, and she wore a black turtleneck. She called for Butch and he came to the door in a dark green work shirt and stained jeans. His hair was grayer than I'd remembered, or maybe I just wasn't used to seeing him without a hat. I could hear the TV on somewhere behind him. He looked surprised but in no real way distressed to see me. He told his wife to bring me a glass of water, and while I drank it he put a hand on my shoulder—I don't know if this was to stabilize me physically or mentally—and then gave me a look that meant, *Well?* He kept glancing off over my shoulder, as if I might have been trailed.

I told him, in what must have been the clumsiest and least lucid string of sentences ever assembled, what it was I needed to do.

"And you're sure this'll do something for you," he said.

"I think so."

He nodded, nodded again, and then went to the closet for his coat. A person's quality is inversely proportional to the quantity of explanation he demands before agreeing to help a friend in need.

It was Butch's idea, once we were in his truck, for us to pick up his son. Bryce might have some better tools, Butch said, plus he was stronger than either one of us. There was an apple in a bag on the dashboard—this might have been another provision from his wife—and while we drove Butch insisted that I eat it; I had to stop myself from eating the core.

Bryce only lived five minutes away, in a one-story house with an aboveground plastic pool in the yard. He climbed into the car, after a short conversation with Butch and a rummage through his own truck. I hadn't been in this car, I realized, or seen Butch's son, since the day we'd found Hannah. Those hands of Bryce's had been the first ones to touch her. None of us talked, except to murmur slightly when a deer ran across the road. We pulled into the driveway at Wright, the flatbed clattering with shovels, just at the point when it was getting cold enough to see your breath. I led them back through the yard and into the woods and over to the clearing where the Wrights were buried. The ground was covered in feathery gray leaves. The gravestones looked like crooked front teeth.

"So we're gonna do this," Bryce said.

It wasn't really a question, but I nodded. *I don't know how but Wright did please help me please.* "Well," Butch said, "*something's* needed doing for a long time."

He went and pulled his truck into the yard, so he could shine his headlights on our work; Bryce disappeared for a while and then came back with a pickaxe, a cluster of shovels, and a few pairs of yellow work gloves.

If your only experience with hole digging comes from sand-castle moats, or from burying tulip bulbs, then you can't possibly understand what it was like digging our way to Wright's coffin. The ground was almost frozen, for one thing, which meant that once we'd cleared away the leaves, we spent the first couple of hours of work—*hours*—smashing away at the grave with the pickaxe and shovels. Having never held a pickaxe before, this was, for a few minutes, satisfyingly brutal work. But cold ground, especially cold ground embedded with roots and stones, is an astonishingly unyielding substance. We pounded and pounded, dug and dug, and only communicated via grunts and nods, shifting around each other occasionally, kneading our arms, flexing our hands. For the first time in days, I wasn't cold. I had taken off my wool coat and pushed the sleeves of my shirt up almost to my shoulders. Butch's shirt was soaked with sweat. Bryce had taken off both of his shirts—his physique was like a carny's, somehow—and now steam was rising off of his actual skin. Still, by nine o'clock, when the moon was racing to the peak of the sky like a white balloon someone had lost hold of, we had succeeded only in making a hummocky mess of the grave's top layer. By ten we had dug out maybe another foot and I had done something to my right shoulder that sent a searing, unmistakably nerve-related pain across the entire length of my back with every stroke.

But desperation—the conviction that someone you love's well-being depends on your finishing—is an astonishing task-master. I thought I'd known determination from music, or from college papers written the night before they were due, but these had been nothing, Christmas lights beside bonfires. So with my burning shoulder, and with popped blisters underneath both of my gloves, and with Butch and his son working just as hard on either side of me, I dug. And dug. And dug. There's a hypnotic aspect to any action that you repeat for long enough; I was actually in more pain, I realized, whenever I stopped digging. The hole was taking on an impressive shape, with walls that barely tapered. It was midnight and then it was one in the morning, and we were down, finally, in the heart of the ground, deep enough that someone could have hurt themselves by stumbling in. And we were getting better at it, too; I was, anyway. Sometimes I stabbed the point of the shovel into the wall of the hole in order to dislodge a rock or to cut through a root. Sometimes I focused on flinging out the backfill. The ground gets softer after the first few feet, it turns out. And body pain transforms itself eventually into a scary sort of lightness—not that it ever became easy, exactly, but just that exhaustion stopped being something I was struggling against and started being the mildly acidic substance in which I was floating. I was in a kind of fugue when Butch finally said, "I think we've got to stop for the night." His son was up at the truck, drinking something from a thermos.

We climbed out—Butch pulled me by the wrist—and we were standing near the edge of the woods when Butch said he wanted to tell me something. I thought, from the way he was looking at me, that he might be about to hug me.

"Hannah asked me a question a week before she died," he said. "About the Kemps. Said she wanted to know if I knew anything more about what happened. I told her I didn't."

I nodded.

"It wasn't true," he said. He wasn't looking at me while he spoke. "I never told anybody this. A little bit before Mrs. Kemp disappeared, my brother told me something that one of the Kemp girls, Marjorie, had told him. Mrs. Kemp had started seeing her future, he told me. Having visions every night of herself as an old lady. It was driving her crazy, Marjorie said. I should have told Hannah that."

"It's—" I started to say, meaning to express that it was okay, that it wouldn't have made any difference, that he'd done enough.

But he wouldn't hear of it. Bryce appeared from the other side of the truck and draped his T-shirt over his shoulder before giving me, or the grave, a half salute. Butch plunged his shovel into the dirt as if it were a bayonet. They both shook my hand and climbed in the car.

I never really considered giving up for the night after they pulled away. I understood, I think, that I was down to my last days, or even hours, at the museum and so I'd better not put anything off. My shoulder had stiffened up, just in the time that I'd been standing by their truck, so I had to do most of the rest of the digging with my left arm. It was harder to see without Butch's headlights but I knew the hole more or less by feel now. I would work at one end for half an hour and then move over and even things up at the other. There was much less left to do than I would have thought, anyway; I wondered if Butch had somehow known this.

My shovel tapped wood for the first time just before it started to get light out, or just when the darkness started to have an edge of blueness to it that I guess was the pre-roll for its getting light out. The hole couldn't have been much deeper than four feet by then, so at first I thought it was another rock, an enormous smooth rock that I would now have to lever out, jumping and jumping on my blade, but I leaned closer and I saw the grain of the wood, the splinteriness of it, and I had to struggle not to fall over. It took until full-on sunrise, an oil spill of color behind the woods, for me to get the coffin's whole surface exposed. It was a no-nonsense coffin: solid as an oak door, with black metal handles on the sides. I tossed my shovel up out of the pit. Until right that minute, I realized, I hadn't fully reckoned with what I was going to do. It turns out that you can distinguish the heart racing caused by exertion and the heart racing caused by terror, even when both are going on simultaneously.

I pried open the lid—it came away easier than I expected, because the hinges had fallen off—and the first thing that struck me was the smell, which was … intense, complicated, *yellow* somehow, but not unbearable, just dense with the information that I shouldn't be there. I was standing straddling the coffin now, leaning down over it like it was some sort of horrible bassinet. It was full of brown stringy tatters, a whole layer of them, and it took me a minute to realize that these must have been Wright's clothes, or a fabric that he'd been wrapped in. I wondered if his body had somehow been shredded too, if this was all that was left of him. I was breathing hard, and entirely through my mouth. I dug gently through the tatters for a minute, an activity like clearing away packing peanuts. And then I froze (even through gloves it was unmistakable): I'd touched bone. I've thought since then how it is that I don't have a better visual memory of that first moment of glimpsing Wright's body, his skeleton, but it was still semi-dark down there, and I was averting as much of my attention as it was possible to do without actually closing my eyes. I do remember the position of his hands, right over left, and the surprising length of his finger bones. And I remember accidentally shifting him at one point, nudging him with the back of my hand, and realizing that his body, what there was of him, was as light as if it had been made of straw. But I barely had to touch his body, once I'd finished clearing the tatters away, because there beside his head (all I remember about the skull is the size of the eye sockets) was a long wooden box with a brass pattern inlaid. I knew—the thing that been steering me all night knew—that this was what I'd been looking for.

With the box in my hands (it was covered in a thick gray dust that I realized might not have been dust), I started scrabbling my way out of the hole, and only then did I allow myself to feel the full horror of where I was and what I was doing. I imagined the dirt sliding in on me; I imagined one of those bony hands shooting out to grab my ankle. But the unprofessionality of my digging, the many dirt chunks and half roots I'd left in place, made for relatively easy climbing. I used my elbows to brace myself against the lip of the hole. Like a grave robber (actually there's no *like* about it), covered in sweat and dirt and God knows what else, I climbed out into the cold gray dawn.

1. Can you list five experiences from your own life that were painful? Please be as detailed as possible. [After five minutes, have three students read aloud items from their lists.]

2. Can you list five experiences from your own life that were pleasurable? Please be as detailed as possible. [After five minutes, have three students read aloud items from their lists.]

3. What do you notice about the painful and pleasurable experiences that you have just heard your classmates share? Were any of the items the same? Do you think any two people would have exactly the same lists as each other? [Call on three to four students.]

4. Why do you think someone would decide to make lists like these? Did writing your lists make you feel silly? Happy? Scared? [Call on three to four students.]

5. Based on what you learned today, do you think that Edmund Wright felt more pain or more pleasure in his life? Do you think most people's lists, if they worked on them for as long as he did, would look like his? [Call on three to four students.]

. . .

4

I spent that entire day, from sunrise to sunset, reading. Except reading doesn't seem like an adequate word to convey the involvement of it—I was prying apart decomposing pages, studying lines of faded ink, filling up the blank parts of Hannah's notebook with notes of my own. The box from Wright's coffin had been full, as I'd hoped it would be, with notebooks—ones with blue-board covers just like the ones in the display cases upstairs. For hours I lay there on the wood floor in the parlor by the fireplace (I'd built another smoky little fire), getting closer to Wright than any Wrighter had ever been.

The story that the notebooks told was discontinuous—notes, with pages missing, were tucked between letters from years earlier; random scraps of journal entries were scattered throughout—but I was able to piece it together, for the most part. The papers had kept surprisingly well in their box, much better than his body had. Making sense of the handwriting was probably the biggest hurdle, and that turned out to be less a matter of word-by-word deciphering than of making some Magic Eye–like inner adjustment and then just trusting my intuition.

I read Wright's accounts of first being visited by his son's spirit, then the many nights after. I read his journal entries and his letters to his brother and his notes to his wife. I arranged things in chronological piles, whenever I could. I read the notes Wright had written to other scientists, begging for their interest. I read the many notes he'd made to himself about developing a unified model of the spirit world, all of which read like some combination of mythology (reincarnation, ghosts, enchanted objects) and botany (cycles, mechanisms, reactions).

And then finally, in the very last notebook, in an entry dated just three days before Wright's death, I read—with papers stacked everywhere around me like a deranged student—the passage that I'd been looking for.

> *It seems plain to me now that spirits long for nothing so much as to be freed back into the cycle of reincarnation, so that they might resume the proper dance of generations in which the rest of us are engaged. Their attempts to achieve this freedom by inducing despair in the living are, of course, monstrous. Had I the will remaining to pursue it, I would seek out a more benign means of granting them their desire. Among the most promising avenues for exploration seems to me one that may prove rash & impracticable: the wholesale destruction of the setting that lately they haunted . . .*

When I stood up it was already dark out. I didn't so much come up with a plan as I did discover that one was already there. It didn't take me long to gather everything I cared about saving: Hannah's notebook; most of Wright's papers; a couple of things from the house. I laid them all in a pile in the center of the quilt from upstairs and tied it into a sloppy bundle. I didn't feel possessed, but I did feel determined, certain, slightly outside of myself. So this was why I'd come back.

The police were wrong about how the fire got started. At first I just made a torch with a rolled-up piece of newspaper from the basket by the hearth. Then I walked around the room—to the curtains, the green sofa, the yellow wall hanging, tap tap tap. It felt like using a magic wand. Except the fire didn't really catch at first—the curtains and wall hanging just smoked and smoldered. So that was when I "employed an accelerant"—which is to say, remembered the lighter fluid in the garden shed.

Setting a fire—deliberately setting a fire that you mean to get out of control—is so strange and in a way so satisfying. It feels, I imagine, something like urinating all over the floors and walls, or stomping through a palace in muddy shoes: a childish satisfaction, all rules suspended. With the bottle of lighter fluid I walked around the house squirting patterns on the walls, the furniture, the floor. The liquid was lighter than water somehow, almost weightless; and that smell—baseball team barbecues, fat dads sitting around in Father's Day T-shirts. Within seconds of my touching the newspaper torch to the trail of lighter fluid on the dining room floor, the curtains were covered in blue flames.

And small fires converge into large fires; this was another surprise to me. It was noisy, like a pack of animals chomping their way through the bones of the house. The walls in the parlor were popping; the floorboards in the dining room were moaning. I thought, watching flames dance across the kitchen floor, about the grill-readiness test, how the coals should be hot enough that you can bear to hold your hand over them for only five seconds. How do you know what you can bear, though, really? What if you don't have a choice?

Because suddenly the fire in the parlor (a whole new wall had burst into flames) was so hot that my whole body couldn't bear it. It was time to leave the house. So I stumbled backward, meaning to grab my bundle and run, but the wall behind me was on fire now too, and I remembered, when the air started to shimmer, the phenomenon in which entire rooms burst into flames. So I ran toward the front door, only somehow that turned out, as I slapped my way around looking for the knob (the whole entryway was full of smoke), not to be the wall with the front door at all; it was a wall in the kitchen. What a stupid, stupid way to die.

For a second I forgot about Hannah, forgot about Wright; I was just an animal in a fire. I ran—still bearing a heat that I couldn't bear, still clutching my quilt bundle—through a boiling miso soup of smoke to the front hallway, babbling to myself, praying. And now I was at the door (the knob felt like a scorching seat belt buckle), now I was on the porch, now I flung my bundle into the yard, now I was safe.

From outside, once I'd caught my breath—this entailed actual gulping of pure freezing air, like chugging water—the fire didn't look quite so terrifying. Flames were wagging from all the windows on the first floor, smoke was pouring upward, but the house was still itself, everything was still in place, it was hard to believe that that had been the inferno. I could feel heat wafting out toward me; the yard was lit up as if by spotlights. No one had arrived yet—not the neighbors, not the fire department, not the police. I thought-panted, *Dear God please let me not have made a mistake.* I imagined the volunteer firefighters, getting phone calls in their kitchens; the neighbors in front of their TVs, asking each other if they smelled something. There's such weird exhilaration in having done something catastrophic that only you know about. I couldn't stand still. The skin on my face, I only noticed now, felt tight and crackly. The hair on my forearms was singed. My right palm was branded with an imprint of the doorknob.

The fire department finally arrived just as the flames burst through the windows on the second floor; the glass shattered loudly enough that my arms flew to shield my eyes. Some neighbors had showed up by then too, staring from the end of the driveway in their sweatshirts and slippers. Their presence settled me down somehow, gave me focus; my job now was to not be singled out. And I wasn't. I was just another obstacle, a piece of lawn furniture for the firemen to race past with their axes and hoses, another body to ask what the hell had happened.

I could barely hear anyone's voices over the fire and the sirens; it was as bright as a stadium now, the heat was coming in waves. Then, when everyone had been standing there for a while ("No one was even *living* there," one woman kept saying), there was a massive cracking, like a bolt of lightning directly overhead. Everyone, even the firemen, stood back silent for a second. It was the roof. At first the peak just shifted slightly, like a log in the fireplace buckling in the middle, but then, with a steady crashing whose sound seemed somehow out of sync, it gave way completely. Everyone gasped. It was no longer a house on fire; it was a fire with a house in it. The flames were ecstatic, triumphant. The smoke was an upward-running river. *Please please please,* I thought, *let this have been* for *something.*

And this is when, still on my feet, I started to shake; my last clear memory is of the woman next to me shouting that I was having a seizure. Hannah, it all rushed through me like a charge through a key: you, the field, the water, the fear—and then a light I thought might burst me open. I felt like I was levitating with the force of it. *You're free,* I thought, *you're free.*

And it wasn't just you. Here was Jan Kemp standing on the railing of a bridge at night, looking down into swirling water; here was Edmund Wright setting down a bottle on his desk; here was a bird gasping for air while something metal came down from above. This all sounds like it must have taken hours, but it was so condensed somehow, there were dozens of things racing through me every second—a mouse stepping onto a trap; a tree cracking in a storm; an ant stumbling, sick with poison. And I must have been knocked onto my back at some point, because I remember that when I came to, myself again, I was looking up at the smoke against the starry sky. I was confused for a second, thinking it was snowing, before I realized it was ash, and that the flakes were somehow carrying your last message to me: *Goodbye.*

I don't remember being strapped to the stretcher, don't

remember the hospital, don't remember those first days afterward. I just remember something I kept saying to anyone who would listen to me, and how happy it made me: Your own life is terrifying, but *life* is an unending astonishment.

So I'm going to keep living out my particular, unread fate, Hannah—that's my burden, that's my blessing, to stumble blindly on. I do sometimes imagine how it will go the next time, though, and the time after that. We'll be a bald man selling car parts in a Ghanaian market and the brown dog sleeping at his feet; we'll be a glistening silver trout in Montana and the woman puckering to kiss it; we'll be children in a suburb of Paris, seated side by side on the bleachers on their first day of summer camp. I don't worry about whether we'll recognize each other. We're like the hands of a clock, Hannah, chasing and escaping each other, losing and finding each other, around and around, again and again, joined way down at the root, no matter how far apart.

Acknowledgments

Thank you to Doug Stewart, Jenny Jackson, Zakiya Harris, Joshua Van Kirk, Billy Holiday, Sam, Elyse, Nishant, and my parents.

AT THE BOTTOM OF EVERYTHING

It's been ages since the "incident" that estranged former best friends Adam and Thomas, and Adam has long since decided he's better off, even if his own life hasn't exactly turned out as planned. Ten years after the two friends spoke their last words, Adam is working as a tutor, sleeping with the mother of a student, and spending most of his nights looking up his ex-girlfriend on Facebook. But when he receives an e-mail from Thomas's mother begging for his help, he finds himself drawn back into his old friend's world. Thomas hasn't been doing well, and now he's disappeared while traveling in India. As Adam embarks upon a magnificently strange and unlikely journey, Ben Dolnick unspools a tale of friendship, spiritual reckoning, and redemption.

Fiction

YOU KNOW WHO YOU ARE

A gorgeous novel of family life, *You Know Who You Are* is the story of the Vine family: Arthur, Alice, and their three children. The eldest, Will, is well-mannered and academically driven. The youngest, Cara, is a sweet little charmer. Jacob, the middle child, is less sure of who he is. He's funny, he's impulsive, and he is often held hostage by his urges to make chaos. But when their mother, Alice, falls ill, Jacob begins to experiment—guiltily, nervously—with the special freedoms conferred on the motherless. Following the Vines as Jacob moves through high school, college, and beyond, *You Know Who You Are* is a wise, funny, elegiac novel of moving on, pulling together, and answering that most complicated of questions: Who will you decide to become?

Fiction

ZOOLOGY

Zoology is the story of Henry Elinsky, who takes a job at the Central Park Zoo after flunking out of college. Henry discovers that becoming an adult takes a lot more than just a weekly paycheck. "Ben Dolnick is a writer of incredible sensitivity. *Zoology* explores the tricky journey to adulthood with honesty, humor, and generosity" (Jonathan Safran Foer).

Fiction

VINTAGE CONTEMPORARIES
Available wherever books are sold.
www.vintagebooks.com